LIVERPOOL'S
GREATEST MOMENTS

First published in the UK in 2025 by Dino Books,
an imprint of Bonnier Books UK,
5th Floor, HYLO, 105 Bunhill Row,
London, EC1Y 8LZ
www.bonnierbooks.co.uk

X @UFHbooks
www.heroesfootball.com

Text copyright © Studio Press 2025

3 5 7 9 10 8 6 4

All rights reserved. No part of this publication may be reproduced, stored in a retrieval system, or transmitted in any form or by any means, without the prior permission in writing of the publisher, nor be otherwise circulated in any form of binding or cover other than that in which it is published and without a similar condition including this condition being imposed on the subsequent purchaser.

Paperback ISBN: 978-1-78946-903-5

The authorised representative in the EEA is Bonnier Books UK (Ireland) Limited.
Registered office address: Block B, The Crescent Building
Northwood, Santry
Dublin 9, D09 C6X8
Ireland
compliance@bonnierbooks.ie

The views in this book are the author's own and the copyright, trademarks and names are that of their respective owners and are not intended to suggest endorsement, agreement, affiliation or otherwise of any kind.

This book is unofficial and unauthorised and is not endorsed by or affiliated with Liverpool F.C.

A CIP catalogue record for this book is available from the British Library
Printed and bound in Great Britain by Clays Ltd, Elcograf S.p.A

TOM PALMER

ULTIMATE FOOTBALL HEROES

LIVERPOOL'S GREATEST MOMENTS

FROM THE PLAYGROUND
TO THE PITCH

DINO

ULTIMATE FOOTBALL HEROES

Tom Palmer is the author of 58 books for children, including six prize-winning WWI and WWII novels and four football series, *Roy of the Rovers*, *Football Academy*, *Foul Play* and the *Soccer Diaries*. He works in schools up and down the UK promoting reading for pleasure through football. www.tompalmer.co.uk

Cover illustration by Dan Leydon.
To learn more about Dan, visit danleydon.com
To purchase his artwork visit etsy.com/shop/footynews
Or just follow him on X @danleydon

For Stephen McGann, Liverpool fan

THIS BOOK IS FOR YOU

You might be a Liverpool F.C. fan. You might not. Either way, this is my attempt to tell the story of one of the world's foremost football clubs through its 100 greatest moments. Great moments every football fan should know about.

And soon... you will!

Liverpool have had a lot of great moments. As someone who has seen Liverpool legends like Kevin Keegan, Kenny Dalglish and Ian Rush on the pitch and in person, it has been an honour to write this book.

What a history!

If you are a Liverpool fan, it is likely that I have missed one of your great moments. A more personal one? Maybe you went to one of the victory parades for one of the trophies listed here? Maybe you were sat in your front room at home and jumped off the sofa when a goal went in or when a final whistle blew?

But there are so many great moments to choose

from with Liverpool, I'd need to write three or four books to do justice to the club's history.

There's another thing to tell you, too. I've written the book backwards. We begin in 2025, not 1892.

I've ordered it this way because I thought you'd like to read about what you know most about first – Mo Salah, Jürgen Klopp, Alisson Becker – and head back through Liverpool's 20 English league championships, the six European cups... right back to the formation of the club.

But if you don't like what I've done... you can always read it back to front.

Tom

CHAMPIONS OF ENGLAND. AGAIN.

English Champions # 20

On 25 April 2025 Liverpool lined up against Tottenham Hotspur at Anfield, needing a draw to be named English champions.

In front of their loyal fans. At their home stadium, Anfield.

And to do it for a record-equalling 20th time.

Although Liverpool had won the league just five years before in 2020, that season had been troubled by the Covid-19 pandemic and the fans could not enjoy that glorious moment of becoming champions in person.

In 2025 it would be different.

Anfield was full and more than 60,000 fans were there to witness it, with millions cheering them on around the world.

All fans, regardless of team, were moved by the

singing of 'You'll Never Walk Alone' as they watched the Liverpool players form a huddle on the pitch.

The game?

It ended 5–1. More proof that Liverpool were undeniably the best men's football club in England. Liverpool were champions.

At the end of the season, even though they failed to win any of their last four games, their record was astonishing. A lead of 10 points over their nearest rivals, Arsenal. 25 wins out of 38 games. 84 points and 86 goals scored. Clearly the best team in England. By a long way.

Liverpool had dominated the top flight of the English league throughout the 2024–25 season and had secured their 20th league title, tying at 20–20 with Manchester United. Liverpool's six Champions League wins against Manchester's three meant that Liverpool were now the greatest team in the history of the England game.

You can read about their other 19 league titles and the other thirty or so trophies in the rest of this book, alongside some other marvellous moments in the history of our greatest football team.

LIVERPOOL'S GREATEST MOMENTS

ENGLISH PREMIER LEAGUE								
	P	W	D	L	F	A	GD	Pts
Liverpool	38	25	9	4	86	41	+45	84
Arsenal	38	20	14	4	69	34	+35	74
Man City	38	21	8	9	72	44	+28	71

KEY TO TABLES:
P – games played;
W – games won;
D – games drawn;
L – games lost;
F – for (goals scored);
A – against (goals conceded);
GD – goal difference (difference between goals for and against);
Pts – total points earned by the team in the league

TOP OF THE LEAGUE

English Champions # 20

In winning their 20th league title, Liverpool finally caught up with Manchester United to become one of two teams to have jointly won the most English league titles.

Liverpool had been top of this league of leagues until 2009 when Manchester United joined them on 18 titles, taking over Liverpool as outright leaders with 19 titles in 2011.

Manchester United's supremacy over Liverpool lasted 14 years.

For the record, the top five English title-winning teams of all time are:

LIVERPOOL'S GREATEST MOMENTS

Liverpool	20
Man United	20
Arsenal	13
Man City	10
Everton	9

The 2025–26 season might see Liverpool or Manchester United take a lead with 21 titles.

Based on their performance in 2024–25 it seems likely that the first team to reach 21 will be Liverpool.

But that is all in the future...

GAME CHANGERS

Liverpool Women F.C.

Liverpool women finished the 2024–2025 Women's Super League in seventh position. That is out of twelve teams in the WSL. A solid season with the team established as a top flight team in a season with an exciting end.

The exciting end?

The Lionesses attempting to regain the EUROs during the summer.

Liverpool Women F.C. – as you might know – were instrumental in helping to create a women's league that can deliver a tournament-winning England team. What Liverpool did to help create a professional game in England was a game changer. You will read more about how that all came about later in the book.

Liverpool reached the semi-finals of the FA Cup in 2024–25, losing to the best team in England, Chelsea.

LIVERPOOL'S GREATEST MOMENTS

It was a good season, if not a great season. And one thing Liverpool can take from it is finishing above their local rivals, Everton.

The future is bright for Liverpool F.C. and the Lionesses.

SALAH AND VAN DIJK SIGN CONTRACT EXTENSIONS

Players

There was a point in spring 2025 when it looked like Liverpool were going to lose three of their very best players on free transfers.

The contracts of Trent Alexander-Arnold, Mo Salah and Virgil van Dijk were all coming to an end as the 2024–25 season came to its conclusion. All had been linked with other clubs and none had committed themselves to the future of Liverpool F.C.

To lose three players of that calibre would be very damaging for any football club. To lose them and receive no income for them, worse.

But in April 2025 – as the team stormed towards its 20th league championship – news came from Anfield. Mo Salah had signed a contract extension. Then Van Dijk had done so too.

LIVERPOOL'S GREATEST MOMENTS

Great news for all Liverpool fans.

The future of the club was looking good. Very good.

ARNE SLOT

Manager

In the summer of 2024, when Arne Slot arrived at the AXA Training Centre in Kirkby, Merseyside, there was still a sense of sadness in the air.

Jürgen Klopp was gone. Klopp had been Liverpool manager for nine years and, as well as winning the Champions League and many other major honours, he had made Liverpool F.C. the English Champions, something that only four previous Liverpool managers – Bill Shankly, Bob Paisley, Joe Fagan, and Kenny Dalglish some 30 years earlier – had ever achieved before.

Arne Slot had to follow Klopp. But who is he?

Arne Slot is Dutch. He had been manager of Rotterdam club Feyenoord in the Dutch Eredivisie for three years, winning 98 games out of 150. In a league dominated by Ajax and PSV Eindhoven, Slot had guided Feyenoord to winning the Dutch league and cup, as well as reaching the final of the Europa Conference League.

So he had a pedigree. But would he be good enough to emulate Shankly, Paisley, Fagan, Dalglish and Klopp?

We know the answer to that now. But on 1 June 2024 we had no idea what the Dutchman was capable of.

KLOPP'S LAST TROPHY

League cup # 10

When the teams lined up for the 2024 EFL – or Carabao – Cup final against Chelsea, Liverpool were branded 'Klopp's Kids' by former Manchester United legend, Gary Neville.

It was true Liverpool were being represented by a young team. With Salah, Núñez, Alexander-Arnold and Matip all injured, the line-up was inexperienced – although they still had Virgil van Dijk as captain and Kelleher in goal. And even though Kelleher was a veteran of the 2022 final, he was still the number two Liverpool keeper.

But both Virgil and Kelleher would prove to be match winners.

With 118 minutes gone the game looked like it would be just another 0–0 cup final, with another penalty shootout.

As always, there had been plenty of goal-mouth action between the two rivals:

Chelsea's Raheem Sterling – hoping to haunt his former club – having a goal disallowed, correctly.

Liverpool's Gakpo hitting the post.

Then Virgil van Dijk having a goal disallowed, dubiously.

Next Conor Gallagher hit the post at the other end. And Chelsea were on top, as the game went into extra time. Kelleher had to make two excellent saves from Cole Palmer and Gallagher again, and was doubtless mentally preparing himself to face penalties.

Until the 118th minute. Until a late, perfect corner for Liverpool.

Tsimikas's delivery arrived close to the six-yard line. And there was Virgil van Dijk, leaping to head the ball across the Chelsea keeper into the goal mouth.

One-nil to Liverpool. Job done.

LIVERPOOL 7
MAN UNITED 0

Rivals: Manchester United

At half time – even though they were 1–0 down to a Cody Gakpo strike – Manchester United must still have fancied themselves to get a result at Anfield on 5 March 2023. Unbeaten in 11 matches, United had, the week before, lifted their first trophy for six seasons. It had been a long wait for a team who used to be one of the best in Europe.

But it was not to be. Manchester United were about to get a hammering.

A header from Núñez on 47. A second strike from Gakpo on 50. And then a beauty from Salah, after 66, rifling the ball into the roof of the net, equalling Robbie Fowler's record as Liverpool's leading Premier League scorer with 128 goals.

Then Núñez headed a second. 5–0.

LIVERPOOL'S GREATEST MOMENTS

Two more goals came during the last 10 minutes: Firmino finishing things off to make it 7–0. But it was the sixth goal that created history for Mo Salah. His reflex six-yard shot took him to 129 Premier League goals and a new record for Liverpool.

And it was a day for a club record too. This was the biggest win in the fixture between Liverpool and their most bitter rivals, outdoing Liverpool's 5–0 win at Old Trafford the previous season, and their 7–1 victory in the 1895–96 season.

ALISSON SCORES, AGAIN

League Cup # 9

The 2022 Carabao (EFL) Cup final went down in history as including the most exciting goalless cup final and the most dramatic penalty shootout in English cup history.

It was the first of two cup finals between Liverpool and Chelsea that year. An intense game with dozens of goalmouth incidents. Shots cleared off the line at both ends. Great saves. Terrible misses.

Then Liverpool had a Matip goal disallowed, as Virgil van Dijk pulled Chelsea's Reece James just as the ball was fired into the penalty area.

Not to be outdone, Chelsea scored three goals. All disallowed.

Goalless, the game went into extra time as more great saves were made and even more goal line clearances. The Chelsea keeper, Édouard Mendy was playing wonderfully – and thanks, partly to him, the game remained at 0–0 after 120 minutes. So: penalties.

But... just before the penalty shootout – Chelsea took off Mendy, their first choice keeper, and brought on Kepa, their penalty-saving expert.

What happened next was extraordinary. Like a cautionary tale for the Chelsea management. Because all 10 outfield players took a penalty from each side. And all of them scored, including Milner, Robertson and Jota, beating the so-called penalty expert, Kepa.

With no outfield players left to take penalties, the Liverpool keeper for the day, Alisson Becker, stepped up to take Liverpool's 11th penalty. And scored.

Now Kepa had to score to keep Chelsea in the game.

But he missed.

And so, Liverpool lifted their ninth league cup.

POOR THOMAS TUCHEL

FA Cup # 8

On 14 May 2022, the then-Chelsea manager, Thomas Tuchel, surely felt that today would be the day when he would get what he deserved: when he would become the first German manager to win the English FA Cup.

Tuchel's hopes must have been raised when both Virgil van Dijk and Mohamed Salah went off, injured, for Liverpool. Without two of their best players, Liverpool were weaker. Weren't they?

But when the game ended 0–0 after extra time, Tuchel must have had flashbacks to the EFL Cup final back in February, when Liverpool had defeated his Chelsea team after eleven penalties each. Could it happen again? Could he leave Wembley for a third time within a year as a loser?

With the penalty count level at 5–5, Chelsea's

young England international, Mason Mount, stepped up to take an excellent penalty towards the bottom left corner of Alisson's goal. But somehow Alisson Becker reached the ball, pushing it away with a strong left wrist.

Tuchel may have wanted to look away as Liverpool's Kostas Tsimikas stepped up to take his penalty. He had to miss… but he didn't, slotting the ball to the right as the Chelsea keeper dived the other way.

While the Liverpool players and fans celebrated another trophy, Thomas Tuchel looked disconsolate. He walked up the Wembley steps to collect another loser's medal.

Liverpool had won their eighth FA Cup.

RIVALS: CHELSEA

Although Liverpool's most famous rivalries are with Manchester United and neighbours Everton, the 21st century has seen them develop a lively rivalry with Chelsea. On the pitch and off it.

Liverpool took pole position in the rivalry with their two cup wins in 2022.

On the pitch the two clubs had now played each other in six major cup finals between 2005 and 2024. Liverpool won two EFLs, one FA and one UEFA super cup, while Chelsea won an FA and an EFL.

In the Champions League the two clubs faced each other in five consecutive seasons. They drew twice in the group stages in 2005–06, and each team won twice in the knockout quarter- and semi-finals between 2004–05 and 2007–08.

Liverpool has the edge in that, they have also won two of the three semi-finals they competed in, compared with Chelsea's one.

But perhaps what really added fuel to the fire of this rivalry were three events which had nothing to do with winning and losing.

The first event concerned Liverpool golden boy, Fernando Torres. Torres, a Spanish international striker, had been at Liverpool for three years, scoring a remarkable 81 goals in 142 games. He was lethal. The Kop loved him. The city loved him. But in 2011, he signed for Chelsea for £50m, a British transfer record fee. Liverpool fans were not happy, waving flags saying 'traitor' at Torres when he made his debut for Chelsea at Stamford Bridge, and shouting worse insults.

Then, two years later, in 2013, another Liverpool legend, Luis Suárez – playing in a Premier League game at Anfield and tussling for the ball in the penalty area – grabbed the Chelsea defender Branislav Ivanovic... and sank his teeth into his arm. It was not spotted by the referee, but fans in the stadium and on TV saw it. Chelsea fans were furious. Suárez remained on the pitch and went on to score a late equaliser that would never have happened, had he been sent off. Chelsea fans were even more furious.

Finally, in 2014, with Liverpool top of the league and heading for their first English title for a quarter of a century, team captain, Steven Gerrard slipped inexplicably as he received a pass in injury time, allowing Chelsea forward Demba Ba to take the ball and score. It was a hammer blow for Liverpool's title chances.

A proper rivalry. On and off the pitch.

CHAMPIONSHIP PROMOTION

Back in the WSL

As you will read about later in this book, Liverpool Women won the Women's Super League in 2013 and 2014.

But after that, things went less well. The coach who led them to that success – Matt Beard – left the club and the owners did not invest in the women's team as well as they should have.

And so... Liverpool F.C. Women were relegated from the top flight in 2020.

But they were to bounce back, showing real character.

After just missing out on promotion in 2020–21, and with the club keener to back their women's team, Matt Beard was reappointed manager. He returned in May 2021, giving him time to prepare for the 2021–22 season.

And, in his first season back, Liverpool lifted the Championship trophy, the second tier of English women's football. They won 16 out of their 22 games, losing only twice.

After returning to the top flight, Liverpool's next two seasons saw them finishing in seventh place, then fourth, in the Women's Super League.

WOMEN'S SUPER LEAGUE 2021–22								
	P	W	D	L	F	A	GD	Pts
Liverpool	22	16	4	2	49	11	+38	52
London	22	13	2	7	35	22	+13	41
Bristol City	22	11	4	7	43	28	+15	37

ALISSON SCORES

Player

It was May 2021 and – after a season delayed by Covid – Liverpool needed to win their last three games to have a chance of qualifying for the Champions League.

Could they do it?

It seemed unlikely.

The first of their three vital games was at West Brom. After 95 minutes the score was 1–1. The dream of the Champions League was almost dead.

Then Liverpool won a late, late corner. As the teams were taking their positions, a strange figure appeared in the West Brom penalty area. Dressed in black from head to foot. Exceptionally tall.

It was Alisson Becker. Liverpool's Brazilian keeper. A man who had recently lost his father in a tragic drowning accident back in Brazil. A man who was determined to keep the Champions League dream alive.

The corner was played into the penalty area. The ball reached Alisson. Who headed it home.

It was quick. It was simple. It was a miracle.

Alisson was Liverpool's first keeper to score in open play in their entire history. Wild celebrations. On the pitch and for Liverpool fans watching at home. Liverpool led 2–1.

In a rare interview after the game, Alisson said he felt that 'God had placed his hand on my head.'

Liverpool went on to win their last two games against Burnley and Crystal Palace to finish third, and so qualified for the Champions League.

CHAMPIONS AGAIN, AT LAST

English Champions # 19

The painful 30-year wait for Liverpool to be named Champions of England – and their first Premier League title – looked to be over, as the 2019–20 football season game neared its climax.

A team featuring Mo Salah and Virgil van Dijk, and captained by Jordan Henderson, had won 27 of their first 29 games. They were by far the best team in England.

But – even though Liverpool had a huge lead and had been top of the league since August – it could have all come to nothing.

Because Covid happened.

All public gatherings were banned. No football. For three months. It was possible the whole season could be declared void! It looked like Jürgen Klopp's team could be denied the English Championship, unlike

Shankly's, Paisley's, Fagan's and Dalglish's teams.

After some agony... it was decided the football season would begin again three-and-a-half months later.

Despite the delays, Liverpool F.C. finally cruised to victory and were named champions of England for the first time in 30 years.

But it was not the celebration it could have been. The games were all played behind closed doors. Covid had seen to that. And, because public gatherings were still discouraged, fans could not celebrate in bars.

Most Liverpool fans had to celebrate in their front rooms with their families, making memories that will live with them forever.

ENGLISH PREMIER LEAGUE, 2019-2020								
	P	W	D	L	F	A	GD	Pts
Liverpool	38	32	3	3	85	33	+52	99
Man City	38	26	3	9	102	35	+67	81
Man United	38	18	12	8	66	36	+30	66

VIRGIL VAN DIJK

Player

Over the years, the UEFA men's Player of the Year award has been won by the likes of Iniesta, Lewandowski and Haaland. And more than once by Messi and Ronaldo, of course.

The award is chosen by the coaches of the 80 teams who played that season in the Champions League and Europa League and by 55 football journalists, one from each of the UEFA football nations.

Of the top six players in the vote for the 2018–19 season, four were from Liverpool: Mané, Salah, Alisson and van Dijk.

The winner?

Virgil van Dijk.

A great moment for a great player. And for Liverpool F.C.

WORLD CHAMPIONS

FIFA World Club Cup # 1

There have been versions of a world club football tournament for decades. The version now played – organised by FIFA – started in 2000. It features football teams that have won major continental trophies from every football federation across the world:

Africa. Asia. CONCACAF. Europe. Oceana. South America.

In 2019, Liverpool played in their second World Club Cup finals. They lost at their first attempt. Could the Anfield club finally become the best football club team in the world?

In the semi-final it took an extra-time ninety–first-minute winner from Firmino for Liverpool to beat Mexican team, Monterrey. The Brazilian had set up a final with the legendary football team from his home country, Flamengo.

And so, to the game that Liverpool needed to win, to be able to say, 'We are the best team in the world'. Firmino was seemingly desperate to win it for his English team against his fellow Brazilians.

In the first minute of the first half Firmino, one-on-one with the keeper, lofted the ball over the bar.

In the first minute of the second half, Firmino was there again, his crisp shot hitting the inside of the post and angling behind the keeper's back but still not into the net.

Extra time, 99 minutes on the clock, the tension at fever pitch – and Mané played Firmino into the penalty area.

Firmino in space.

Lots of space.

One touch to put the keeper onto the floor. A second, then a third touch to tie the defender in knots, a twist, a turn and Roberto Firmino slotted the ball home.

One-nil.

Ten minutes later, Liverpool F.C. were the World Club Champions.

CHAMPIONS LEAGUE # 6

The Sixth

After just 24 seconds of the 2019 Champions League Final, Sadio Mané crossed the ball towards the Tottenham goal from the corner of the penalty area. The ball struck Spurs' Moussa Sissoko on the arm.

Penalty!

Unfortunate for Tottenham. Wonderful for Liverpool.

Mo Salah stepped up to slot it home.

One-nil to Liverpool in under a minute. The red ranks of supporters in Atlético Madrid's stadium celebrated.

But, as all football fans know, 1–0 is not a big lead and – as the game played on – that sense of celebration in the stands faded to anxiety. Would Spurs get one back?

The game wore on. Shots going wide. Saves being

made. It was tense. It was tight. Then, after 87 minutes, as Spurs tried more and more risky attacks, there was space at the back. And Liverpool scored again. Receiving a crisp pass, Divock Origi struck it low and hard across the face of the goal, beating the keeper.

Two-nil. Three minutes left. Game over.

And Liverpool were European Champions for the sixth time.

THE COMEBACK

Liverpool 4 Barcelona 0

As greatest moments go, rarely does a semi-final stick in the minds of fans. Especially when they're Liverpool fans, so used to watching their team compete in finals.

But they remember their astonishing victory against Barcelona in 2019.

They had lost at the Bernabéu. Three-nil. No Lionel Messi team could give up a three–nil lead. Could it?

Liverpool needed a strong start. And they got it – Divock Origi scoring after just seven minutes to put hope in the heart of Liverpool fans.

The camera zoomed in on Lionel Messi. His face betrayed any sense of anxiety. Could Liverpool do it? He probably knew that, if any team could, Liverpool could.

Anfield was packed and millions of Liverpool fans were watching on TV as they roared on their team.

But at half time the score remained 1–0. Liverpool were losing 3–1 on aggregate, with only 45 minutes to go.

Andy Robertson came off at half time to be replaced by Georginio Wijnaldum. Thanks to that substitution, just 10 minutes later Liverpool were 3–0 up on the night, and level at 3–3 on aggregate.

Breathtaking.

Two Wijnaldum goals. Two goals in two minutes. The first, a neat right-footer from a cross from the right. The second, a strong header from a cross from the left.

Anfield exploded and the camera focused in on Messi again. His face of anxiety had changed to one of anger. Could this really happen to him? To Barcelona?

With 79 minutes on the clock, a corner for Liverpool, Trent Alexander-Arnold winning it by clipping the ball of a Barcelona defender.

This is the moment that sticks in the memories of those Liverpool fans in Anfield that night and the millions watching on the TV. Alexander-Arnold places the ball for the corner, takes three steps away from the ball, as if he is not going to take it, then he doubles back and – with the whole Barcelona team ball watching – Alexander-Arnold fires the ball across the pitch to an unmarked Divock Origi on the edge of the six-yard box.

Origi sticks the ball in the net and Liverpool are 4–3 up on aggregate.

When the final whistle goes Messi leaves the pitch, head down, fuming. And Liverpool? They go on to play Tottenham in the final.

UNLAWFUL

April 2016

In 1989, 96 Liverpool fans were killed in a terrible disaster at Hillsborough football stadium in Sheffield. At the time a lot of the media – notably *The Sun* newspaper – blamed the Liverpool fans for causing the deaths.

The 1990 Taylor Report into the disaster did blame the Liverpool fans for the disaster, but it did say that Liverpool fans being drunk and without tickets were secondary factors.

But in 2012 the Hillsborough Independent Panel concluded that Liverpool fans had been in no way to blame for those deaths. The courts were then encouraged by the tenacity of the victims' families to decide who really *was* to blame.

In 2016 – after a 27-year campaign by the victims' families – the blame was at last shifted from the fans to the police, the ambulance service and Sheffield Wednesday's Hillsborough Stadium.

The verdict found that the match commander – Chief Superintendent David Duckenfield – was responsible for manslaughter and gross negligence. And that other errors by the police caused a dangerous situation at the turnstiles and on the terraces. Also, that Hillsborough Stadium was not well prepared enough for the game – on the day or in the lead-up to the day. And that the police and ambulance service had delayed declaring the incident a major incident, which led to a delay in responses from emergency services, and the deaths of many more fans who were not reached in time.

These events do not speak of a great moment. Those terrible and terrifying deaths were a tragedy.

But the determination of the victims' families to get justice that led to the real truth coming out – that is a campaign that Liverpool fans old and young should be proud of.

THE NORMAL ONE

Manager

Jürgen Klopp arrived at Anfield to become Liverpool manager on 8 October 2015. A moment that was to change the course of the history of Liverpool F.C.

He replaced manager, Brendan Rodgers. Rodgers's team had begun the Premier League season poorly. They were an average team. So, after a draw with Everton and a record of one win in the last 10 games left Liverpool in 10th place, Rodgers was sacked.

The club needed a new manager. Someone who would reassert Liverpool as one of the best teams in England, in Europe, in the world.

Since the exceptional 2004–05 season – over a decade ago – Liverpool had won just one trophy: a league cup. The owners and the fans wanted more. They wanted success. When would Liverpool be champions of England again? It had been a quarter of a century since they had matched the kind of success they achieved time after time in the 1970s and 1980s.

So, the Liverpool F.C. owners turned to Jürgen Klopp – a manager with a great track record in German football, twice winning the Bundesliga and once reaching the Champions League final with Borussia Dortmund.

But, as with most managers coming from abroad, many fans did not know a great deal about him.

At Jürgen Klopp's first press conference, he was asked who he was and what he was like. Aware that José Mourinho called himself 'the special one', Klopp declared who he was:

'The normal one,' he said with a smile.

Liverpool fans liked this. Here was a man for whom football was not about his personality or his ego, but about the club. Their club. Liverpool.

Under Jürgen Klopp's guidance, Liverpool would go on to win nearly all the major trophies that a club could win – the Champions League, the UEFA Super Cup, the FIFA World Club Cup, the FA Cup, the League Cup – and he would be the first manager for 30 years to lead Liverpool to become English champions once again.

LUIS SUÁREZ STAYS

Player

The moment when Uruguayan international, Luis Suárez, changed his mind and chose to stay on at Liverpool for the 2013–14 season, led to his winning almost every award that one player could win in one season.

Suárez had asked for a move at the end of the 2012–13 season. He said that Liverpool had promised he could leave if the club did not qualify for the Champions League. He also said he did not like the media attention he and his family were receiving in the UK. The club refused to let him leave, with his manager, Brendan Rodgers, saying he had showed the club great disrespect. He was ordered to train separately from the rest of the squad – though the fans still expressed their love for him.

Not great. Luis Suárez was an outsider.

But something changed to keep Suárez at the club. He was quoted in a Uruguayan newspaper, explaining: 'For now, due to all of the people's affection, I will be staying.'

It was the fans that would keep Luis Suárez at Liverpool. The following season, Luis Suárez scored 31 goals in 37 appearances for Liverpool and won:

- Premier League Player of the Season
- Premier League Golden Boot
- European Golden Shoe (shared with Cristiano Ronaldo)
- PFA Players' Player of the Year (as well as being in the team of the year)
- PFA Fans' Player of the Year
- Football Writers' Association Footballer of the Year
- Football Supporters' Federation Player of the Year

WSL #2

WSL Champions again

Liverpool began the last day of Women's Super League 2014 in mid-table, placed third out of eight teams, and only a freak set of results would allow them to reclaim the WSL title they had won the year before.

What unfolded would become the most exciting final day of the Women's Super League to date.

The table looked like this at the start of play:

WOMEN'S SUPER LEAGUE 2014			
	P	GD	Pts
Chelsea	13	+8	26
Birmingham	13	+6	24
Liverpool	13	+6	23

All three games were coming to an end simultaneously. Chelsea were losing 2–1 at Man City. Birmingham were drawing 2–2 with Notts County. Liverpool – thanks to goals from Natasha Dowie, Lucy Bronze and Fara Williams – were 3–0 up.

As the games moved into injury time, the table looked like this:

WOMEN'S SUPER LEAGUE 2014			
	P	GD	Pts
Liverpool	13	+9	26
Chelsea	13	+7	26
Birmingham	13	+6	25

Just one goal rescuing a draw for Chelsea would make them champions of England with 27 points, and just one goal for Birmingham would give them a win and 27 points.

No more goals were scored. Liverpool F.C. Women became champions of England for the second year on the trot.

This is the final table, in full detail:

WOMEN'S SUPER LEAGUE 2014								
	P	W	D	L	F	A	GD	Pts
Liverpool	14	7	5	2	19	10	+9	26
Chelsea	14	8	2	4	23	16	+7	26
Birmingham	14	7	4	3	20	14	+6	25

JAMIE CARRAGHER

Player

On 19 May 2013 any fans who were inside Anfield will remember seeing Jamie Carragher's guard of honour.

A guard of honour is when a player or manager walks out of the tunnel onto the pitch, and players from both clubs stand on either side of him as he or she walks out to the adulation of the crowd.

With his daughter and his son beside him, Carragher walked out to thousands of fans singing 'We all dream of a team of Carraghers', the defender's song sung to the tune of 'Yellow Submarine'.

A song about a Liverpool man sung to the tune of a song sung by the ultimate Liverpool band, the Beatles.

Why were the Liverpool fans awarding Jamie Carragher this rare honour?

Jamie Carragher was a one-club man. Although he

was brought up as an Everton fan, he only ever played for one club: Liverpool.

He played 737 times for the club, a total second only to Ian Callaghan.

Carragher won one Champions League, one UEFA cup, two UEFA Super Cups, an FA Cup and a League Cup. Sadly, though, he never managed to be part of one of the many Liverpool teams who won the English Championship.

Loved by the fans for being a one-club man, he also championed the club and the city. Although he once said he avoided talking politics, when it came to speaking about the Hillsborough tragedy and how the city of Liverpool was so badly treated by the media and the establishment, he said: 'We stand up for each other… this city doesn't allow people to walk all over it.'

GEMMA BONNER

Player

In November 2023 Gemma Bonner was presented with a framed shirt by the footballer who had played the most games for the Liverpool F.C. men's team, Ian Callaghan.

Bonner had recently clocked up 135 appearances as defender for Liverpool F.C. Women and now joined club legend, Callaghan, as the player who had played the most times for her club, overtaking the previous record holder, Ashley Hodson.

Bonner stands out as a player with the club, but not just because she has played the most times for Liverpool. It was also because of what she was part of, a decade earlier.

When Liverpool F.C. Women won the Women's Super League in 2013 and in 2014, Gemma Bonner was captain. She was brought in to lead the team by head coach, Matt Beard, who had signed her from Chelsea where he had previously worked with her.

Bonner – who began her career at her hometown club, Leeds – said she joined the Reds because she was 'greatly influenced by the commitment that Liverpool F.C. are showing to women's football'. In 2013, Liverpool were the first team to offer their women players full-time professional contracts.

And it was during her time at Liverpool that she was selected for the first of her 12 England caps.

WSL CHAMPIONS

WSL # 1

Liverpool F.C. Women became English champions for the first time in 2013. And what they achieved was quite astonishing. Because in the first two seasons of the Women's Super League, Liverpool had finished bottom of eight teams.

So, why did Liverpool suddenly become a force in the game?

First, they had recently appointed the former Chelsea manager, Matt Beard. Beard had brought in several new players including, from his former club, Gemma Bonner, and the US international, Whitney Engen.

Second, the club had also made some changes off the pitch, with a move from their Skelmersdale Stadium to the Halton Stadium in Widnes.

Most significantly, though, Liverpool had become the first team in England to offer women professional contracts. This was groundbreaking and made Liverpool the trailblazers in professionalising the English women's game.

It was all change off the pitch and in the dressing room. But would it play out differently on the pitch? Could Liverpool avoid bottom spot again?

The answer was yes. Emphatically.

Liverpool turned the table upside down by winning 12 of their 14 games that season, and losing only twice.

Like the men's team had done many times, Liverpool F.C. Women were now the champions of England.

WOMEN'S SUPER LEAGUE 2013								
	P	W	D	L	F	A	GD	Pts
Liverpool	14	12	0	2	46	19	+27	36
Bristol Academy	14	10	1	3	30	20	+10	31
Arsenal*	14	10	3	1	31	11	+20	30

*Arsenal docked three points for fielding an unregistered player.

HE AIN'T HEAVY, HE'S MY BROTHER

Remembering

On 17 September 2012 something happened at Everton's Goodison Park – the home of the enemy – that stands out as a great moment.

Five days earlier the Hillsborough Independent Panel had found that Liverpool fans were in no way responsible for the disaster that killed 96 Liverpool fans. (In 2021 this number became 97 after the death of another fan who died as a result of what happened at Hillsborough.) This refuted and silenced the dreadful slurs that had laid the blame on the Liverpool fans.

Before Everton's next home game, the club from the blue half of the city held, in the words of commentator Jim Rosenthal, 'an act of Remembrance'.

It began with two children at the centre of the pitch. A girl in a blue Everton top, with a Number 9 on the back. A boy in the red of Liverpool with a 6 on the back. This made up the number 96, representing those who, up to that point, had lost their lives because of the Hillsborough disaster.

Then – as the names and faces of those 96 fans were displayed on the Everton scoreboard – the club played the Hollies song '*He Ain't Heavy, He's My Brother'* over the speakers.

Those from the families of the victims were present – as were many former Liverpool players and coaches.

It was a great moment that came about as a result of the most appalling moment in the club's history.

But there was still a long way to go – the families of the victims and the greater Liverpool F.C. family wanted justice. They wanted those who were to blame to be held accountable.

There was another battle to fight. But – on this day – Everton F.C. were the best of brothers.

PROFESSIONAL

Liverpool F.C. Women

After finishing bottom of the new Women's Super League in its first two years, 2011 and 2012, the Liverpool manager, Matt Beard, began the 2013 season by declaring: 'The ambition of the club is to be playing in the Champions League and, next year, competing for the title.'

If you had only studied the record books, you would have thought this crazy talk. But something had happened at Liverpool F.C. that had never happened at an English football team before:

Liverpool F.C. Women were going full-time professional.

It is hard to get your head round that, given that at the time, Arsenal – champions of England for nine years on the bounce – trained only twice a week.

So, why was that? Because the players had other

jobs. Football was not their profession. They could not afford to train every day if they were not being paid. They needed to earn a living.

Liverpool's decision changed this way of thinking. In 2013 they invested in their women's team. With that investment they were able to pay all their players and sign twelve new players, six of them from professional leagues abroad.

Liverpool F.C. had led the way. Other WSL teams followed suit. And change began.

ANOTHER GERRARD FINAL

League Cup # 8

Liverpool captain Steven Gerrard – after lifting the League Cup in 2012 – said that he had mixed feelings about winning. Something that would be explained by the last kick of the game.

After extra time the final score was 2–2, with goals from Martin Škrtel and Dirk Kuyt for Liverpool.

The final would be decided on penalties.

Steven Gerrard stepped up to take the first penalty. He hit the target, but the Cardiff keeper got a hand to the low shot and palmed it onto the bar.

It was a shootout where half the penalties were missed.

Nil-nil after one each.

One-nil to Cardiff after two.

One-one after three.

Two-two after four.

After Liverpool had taken their fifth penalty, leading 3–2, Cardiff needed to score.

Anthony Gerrard – Steven's cousin – stepped up, and missed.

After the game Steven said he felt for his cousin, and he felt for Cardiff.

But – regardless of that – Liverpool had their eighth League Cup.

FOUNDER MEMBERS

Women

Liverpool F.C. Women were proud to be one of the eight founder members of the Women's Super League, WSL for short.

The Women's Super League is the top flight of the women's game in England. It replaced the FA Women's Premier League National Division and began in 2011. And Liverpool F.C. were proud to be one of the eight founder members of the WSL, the others being Arsenal, Birmingham, Bristol, Chelsea, Doncaster, Everton, Lincoln and Liverpool.

Liverpool finished bottom of the league in the inaugural season, averaging attendances of 466. Compare that with the crowds they attract now, of sometimes more than 15,000.

But, had it not been for Liverpool and those

other seven pioneering teams, the astonishing growth of the women's game in England would not have been achieved.

TORRES'S FAST 50

Player

World Cup winner, Fernando Torres, was a goal machine at Atlético Madrid, Liverpool, Chelsea and AC Milan. He also played 110 times for his country Spain, scoring 38 goals.

Torres's greatest achievement at Liverpool came on 29 December 2009 when he scored a winning goal against Aston Villa. Three minutes into second-half injury time, Yossi Benayoun put the ball into the path of Torres, who fired a low shot past the Villa keeper.

Torres had scored 50 league goals in a shorter time period than any other Liverpool player, even faster than the likes of Ian Rush, Robbie Fowler and Kenny Dalglish.

FA CUP #7

The Gerrard Final

With a footballer like Steven Gerrard on your team in a cup final you always have a chance. In the final of the 2006 FA Cup, the fans of Liverpool and their opponents, West Ham United, knew this.

After 28 minutes Liverpool were 2–0 down. Not many teams come back from two down in a cup final. But, less than a year since the Miracle of Istanbul, no-one from Merseyside had given up. In the 32nd minute, Djibril Cissé snatched one back for Liverpool, so the half time score was West Ham 2 Liverpool 1.

Then, 10 minutes into the second half, it became 2–2 after fierce half-volley from inside the penalty area from Steven Gerrard.

Cometh the hour, cometh the man.

But 10 minutes after that it was 3–2 – to West Ham. The Londoners were back in the lead. Did Liverpool have the character to come back? Again?

Just as the 90 minutes were up, and the match announcer was telling the crowd how many minutes the referee had added on, the ball bounced out of the area, with nine West Ham defenders between it and the goal.

To Steven Gerrard, 30 yards out.

The ball bounced twice, then Gerrard struck it so hard it didn't touch the ground until it hit the back of the net. It arrowed past the West Ham keeper, Shaka Hislop.

Three-all.

The final was set for extra time – and then penalties. Which Liverpool would win 3–1.

SUPER CISSÉ

With rumours that Liverpool were about to sign back Michael Owen, just one year after he had left for Real Madrid, the existing Liverpool striker, Djibril Cissé, was under pressure. He needed to prove his worth to Liverpool F.C. and to the fans.

He did just that in the UEFA Super Cup final of 2005.

Liverpool were in the final just three months after the Miracle of Istanbul. Their opponents were CSKA Moscow, winners of the 2004–05 UEFA Cup. It was a warm August night in Monaco, but it did not begin well for Liverpool; Daniel Carvalho scored for the Russians midway through the first half.

One-nil to the Russians. With the Liverpool fans singing about Michael Owen in the stands.

Then, after working in the Mediterranean heat for 82 minutes, a long ball from Pepe Reina in the Liverpool goal almost found its way to Cissé. But a CSKA defender got to it first, hitting the ball against

Cissé, ricocheting towards the goal for Cissé to follow it towards the net.

One-all.

Full time. Extra time. And on 103 minutes, Cissé was in again. Another long ball. The Senegalese striker controlled it, found himself one-on-one with the keeper and shot at goal. But somehow the keeper saved it. But the ball came back to Cissé, who took control, twisting his body to fire Liverpool ahead.

At 2–1, Liverpool were in charge. But Cissé was not done yet. Now he turned provider, chasing a third long ball to the corner of the pitch and lofting it into the penalty area for Luis García to head home.

At 3–1, Liverpool had their first trophy of the 2005–06 season – and it was still only August. Cissé was the hero, and the following day Michael Owen signed for Newcastle United.

THE LIVERPOOL FANS

AC Milan 3 Liverpool 0 (at half time)

At half time, the score in the 2005 Champions League final – held in the Atatürk Olympic Stadium, Istanbul – suggested that the game was essentially over.

AC Milan 3 Liverpool 0. Goals from Paolo Maldini (after 50 seconds) and two from Crespo on 39 and 44 minutes. Surely you couldn't come back from a three-goal deficit against a team containing legends like Maldini, Kaká and Andrea Pirlo.

You'd need a miracle.

Was it the greatest moment in the history of Liverpool F.C.?

Probably.

Even the greatest moment in the history of football?

Possibly.

During half time, as the players from both teams

talked and stretched and rested in the changing rooms under the main stand, it was not the players who created greatness. It was the Liverpool fans.

The teams in both changing rooms heard it. That song. The Liverpool F.C. anthem. Louder and louder, filling the stadium, filling the city of Istanbul and beyond: 'You'll Never Walk Alone'.

When the players came out for the second half, the score was the same: 3–0 to the Italians. But something had changed.

THE FIFTH

European Champions # 5

There are so many highlights that you could pick from that night in Istanbul in 2005.

From 3–0 down, Liverpool began to stage an awesome comeback. Each of their three goals – the Steven Gerrard header, the Vladimír Šmicer strike, the Xabi Alonso penalty – were potential moments to savour, as was each penalty scored or saved in the penalty shootout.

At 3–3, the game was into extra time.

One moment in this game's extra time sometimes gets forgotten. Not the fans in red singing 'You'll Never Walk Alone'. Not the players scoring and celebrating goals. Not Rafael Benítez on the touchline orchestrating the ultimate football masterclass.

The great moment – in extra time, anyway – was performed by a man in black.

Jerzy Dudek.

On 117 minutes, with Milan attacking well, Andriy Shevchenko leapt into the air to head home a perfect cross from the left. But somehow Dudek, the Liverpool keeper, parried it away, only for it to fall to Shevchenko's feet again. Three yards out, the keeper on his backside. The Ukrainian hit it hard. But somehow... somehow... Dudek got a hand to it and the ball spun over the crossbar.

Astonishing.

The Miracle of Istanbul was still on.

"I WAS THERE"

Fans

There are never enough tickets for Liverpool games. Home or away, Liverpool could always take more. Most fans just can't get tickets. Most fans couldn't afford to travel to Turkey to watch the Miracle of Istanbul and see Liverpool lift their fifth Champions of Europe trophy.

But tens of thousands could turn out on the streets of the city when Liverpool F.C. brought the trophy home, giving the fans, especially children, the chance to see their heroes – and the Champions League trophy – for real.

The night after they won the European Cup in Istanbul, the Liverpool bus left Anfield at 8 p.m., driving slowly through the streets, with police horses leading the way, and a banner on the front of the bus reading 'LIVERPOOL Champions of Europe 2005'.

LIVERPOOL'S GREATEST MOMENTS

The bus travelled to St George's Hall in the centre of Liverpool, while tens of thousands fittingly sang 'You'll Never Walk Alone'.

This was the moment. This was a night so many fans would remember for the rest of their lives and could say, years later, 'I was there'.

BILLY LIDDELL REMEMBERED

Player

On 4 November 2004 a commemorative plaque was unveiled opposite the Liverpool F.C. Museum at Anfield. It was to remember the Liverpool legend, Billy Liddell, and was unveiled by his widow, Phyllis, and by Ian Callaghan, the man who has played most games for the club.

But who was Billy Liddell? And why him?

Many fans may not have heard of him, especially younger fans. But many have – as was evidenced by a survey done not that long ago.

In 2006 a survey was conducted to find out from the Liverpool fans who were the team's best players in history. It was called *100 Players Who Shook the Kop*. A total of 110,000 fans voted and Billy Liddell came sixth.

This is the top six.

LIVERPOOL'S GREATEST MOMENTS

1	Kenny Dalglish
2	Steven Gerrard
3	Ian Rush
4	Robbie Fowler
5	John Barnes
6	Billy Liddell

But why is Liddell's commemorative plaque on the wall at Anfield? The stats help explain why:

He is the fourth most played player in the league.

He has scored the fourth most league goals.

He was leading scorer for eight seasons out of nine from 1949 to 1958.

He signed for Liverpool in 1938 and left the club in 1961. During the years of the Second World War, he served as a navigator in the Royal Air Force, putting his life on the line to defeat fascism.

That's why.

RAFAEL BENITEZ

Manager

When Rafa Benítez arrived at Liverpool F.C. on 16 June 2004 he was the first Spaniard to manage a team in the English Premier League. As manager at Valencia, he had won La Liga twice in three seasons, as well as the UEFA Cup.

Benítez's pedigree was excellent and one reason he was appointed manager at Liverpool was so they could once again be contenders for the two honours they had once won:

To be champions of Europe for the first time since 1984.

To be champions of England for the first time since 1990.

Winning the English league would have to wait another 16 years, but at least, in his first season, Benitez would manage Liverpool to become

Champions of Europe for the fifth time.

How did he change things?

First, he persuaded Steven Gerrard not to leave the club and play for Chelsea.

Second, he also encouraged Carragher to become a centre back as opposed to a more utility player.

With a knowledge of La Liga, he brought in two Spaniards, Xabi Alonso and Luis García – both players instrumental in the success of the club that season.

On the night of the final in Istanbul he was praised for his calm and methodical approach to overcoming a 3–0 half-time deficit.

Rafa Benítez brought glory back to Liverpool F.C.

LEAGUE CUP # 7

Dudek won it

After Liverpool had beaten Manchester United in the 2003 League Cup final Alex Ferguson said that the Liverpool goalkeeper had won it for them. If you watch the highlights of the game, it's true. So true that the Polish international keeper in question won Man of the Match.

Jerzy Dudek was a hero, saving goal-bound strikes from Sebastián Verón, Paul Scholes and three from Ruud van Nistelrooy.

Inside Cardiff's Millennium Stadium, its closed roof creating a cauldron of noise, Liverpool went on to win their seventh League Cup, called the Worthington Cup at the time.

But it was not just Jerzy Dudek who won the game.

There was also a long-range wonder-strike from Steven Gerrard that looped over the Manchester United keeper, after taking a deflection off a desperate block attempt from David Beckham.

One-nil.

Then – with less than five minutes left and Manchester United pushing for an equaliser – Michael Owen raced free from the defenders and finished it.

Two-nil. The nil being thanks to Jerzy Dudek.

BEATING BAYERN

UEFA Super Cup

The 2001–02 season began how the previous season ended – with another trophy. This was in the UEFA Super Cup, played between the winners of the Champions League (Bayern Munich) and the UEFA Cup (Liverpool).

It was a game won by accurate passing. And pace.

Michael Owen showed both in the 23rd minute, chasing a pass from Steven Gerrard, speeding down the wing, then sliding a perfect pass across the six-yard box for Jon Arne Riise to slot home.

One-nil.

Just before half time, Emile Heskey received the ball with his back to goal, turned, took four touches, positioning himself between a pair of Munich players, and then – with a sudden burst of speed – cut between the two defenders and, in space, clipped the ball home.

Two-nil.

The Germans would come back to score twice in the second half, but not before Michael Owen latched onto the end of a long pass just seconds after the second half had begun, using his famous speed to slice through the Munich defence.

The game ended 3–2 and Liverpool could lift their fifth piece of silverware in the space of just six months.

BALLON D'OR

Player

The Ballon d'Or is awarded to the best footballer in Europe each season, judged by journalists from across the continent. It is a rare honour and, as of 2000, had only been won by three Englishmen: Stanley Matthews, Kevin Keegan twice (both times while at Hamburg SV) and Bobby Charlton.

Only once – in all the club's remarkable history – has a Liverpool player won it.

Michael Owen, in 2001.

Owen recalls being told about the award while in the dressing room before a game. His manager – Gérard Houllier – who was recovering from a serious illness – called him to tell him the news.

Owen remembers not really appreciating what an honour it was, to win the Ballon d'Or. Only later would he understand how big a deal it was to finish above the likes of David Beckham, Thierry Henry, Luís Figo and Zinedine Zidane in the voting that season.

FOWLERBALL

League Cup # 6

The 2001 League Cup final – Liverpool versus Birmingham City – was the first English cup final to be decided on penalties.

But it should be remembered for a goal that could not have been less like a penalty.

When Sander Westerveld, the Liverpool keeper that day, fired a long ball across two-thirds of the length of the pitch, it bounced once before it fell to Robbie Fowler. Fowler turned instinctively and, without allowing the ball a second bounce, he unleashed a powerful shot that flew high over the Birmingham penalty area, then dipped past the fingertips of the Birmingham keeper and under the bar.

Goal. A wonder strike.

After 30 minutes: Liverpool 1 Birmingham 0.

The game stayed at the same scoreline until the

90th minute. But Liverpool just could not keep Birmingham out. They conceded a late penalty that meant they would be forced into extra time.

With no more goals after 120 minutes, for the first time the English cup final was to be decided on a penalty shootout.

After five shots per team, the score was four goals each. Then, after Jamie Carragher scored his spot kick to make it 5–4, Westerveld became the first penalty shootout hero of the new football era, saving off Andrew Johnson and celebrating with his teammates in front of the Liverpool fans.

GOLDEN GOAL

UEFA Cup # 3

The 2001 UEFA Cup Final between Alavés of Spain and Liverpool F.C. was hailed as one of the greatest European finals ever. It saw goals from Markus Babbel, Steven Gerrard, Gary McAllister and Robbie Fowler, cancelled out by a free kick and a hat-trick of Alavés headers from the Spanish team.

Four-all after 90 minutes.

The game would go into extra time. But a different kind of extra time.

Why?

Well, UEFA was experimenting with a new idea: The Golden Goal, meaning whoever scored first in extra time won, at the moment the ball hit the back of the net.

Basically, it was next goal wins. The kind of thing that happened in school playgrounds across the world every weekday.

After 116 minutes, the former Leeds midfielder, Gary McAllister, now seeing his career out at the age of 36 with Liverpool, took a free kick. Whereupon, as the Spanish team had done so many times, an Alavés player headed the ball, directing it into the goal.

Except, this time, the Alavés player had scored against his own team. An own goal.

Five-four to Liverpool.

And Liverpool had won their third UEFA Cup.

THE BOY'S A GENIUS

FA Cup # 6

'When you've got Michael Owen in your team that's what can happen,' the veteran Scottish midfielder, Gary McAllister said after Liverpool's 2–1 victory over Arsenal in the 2001 FA Cup final.

The game had looked like it might be a chastening experience for Liverpool. With seven minutes left the Merseysiders were 1–0 down thanks only to a series of goal-line clearances, mostly from the Finnish international Sami Hyypiä. Without him it could have been 2–0, 3–0 or even 4–0.

But, at the other end of the pitch, Michael Owen was in his prime.

On 83 minutes, McAllister hit a free kick into the Arsenal penalty area. The ball ricocheted around until Owen found the space to power the ball in, angling his body to ensure his fierce shot would beat his England teammate, David Seaman, in the Arsenal goal.

One-one, and barely more than five minutes to go.

The match went on. There was tension now. Would the game go into extra time?

Not with Michael Owen on the pitch.

Another Arsenal attack broke down and – gathering the ball on the edge of his area – Liverpool midfielder, Patrick Berger, took one touch of the ball, looked up, saw Michael Owen and two Arsenal defenders – the only men in the Arsenal half. Berger hit a long ball.

Staying onside until the ball was struck, Owen used his famous pace, speeding between the two Arsenal defenders to take the ball, touch it once, then hammer it across the face of the goal and the outstretched fingers of David Seaman.

Two-one. The Millennium Stadium in Cardiff exploded with noise. Michael Owen had done it. With extraordinary pace. With exceptional accuracy of shot. With skills that would mark Michael Owen out as a Liverpool legend, at the age of just 21.

'The boy's a genius,' the commentator crooned.

JOHN BARNES

Player

John Barnes is considered one of the greatest footballers to play for both Liverpool and for England.

Born in the West Indies, Barnes was 12 when he arrived in the UK. His father was a huge football fan and named his son after the legendary Leeds, Juventus and Wales international player, John Charles.

John spent a decade at Liverpool after signing from Watford in 1987. During that decade, he played alongside club legends including Alan Hansen, Kenny Dalglish, Ian Rush, Robbie Fowler, Michael Owen and Jamie Carragher in teams that won five major honours: two English Championships, two FA Cups and a League Cup. He played 407 times for the club, scoring 108 goals. Quite a record!

At the same time, he played 79 times for England.

It is hard to choose a moment as Barnes's greatest

at Liverpool. There were so many. But one stand-out game came towards the end of the 1995–96 season, between Liverpool and Newcastle, still regarded by some as the greatest Premier League game ever played.

Liverpool, Newcastle and Manchester United were still all competing to be League Champions, and Liverpool had to beat Newcastle to stay in the hunt.

With only minutes left, it was 3–3. Throughout the game, the lead had swapped from one team to the other. Then Barnes dribbled the ball towards the Newcastle area, playing a one-two with Ian Rush. And another. Then, as the ball nearly bobbled out of his control, he knocked an elegant pass out of a cluster of players to Stan Collymore who was storming in from the left.

Collymore met the ball and hammered it home: 4–3.

That goal from Collymore meant that Liverpool could still win the league. But it was the footwork of John Barnes – the passing, the one-twos, the dribbling – that had won the day.

ROBBIE FOWLER

Player

Robbie Fowler was a goal machine. In his first spell at Liverpool, 1993–2001, he scored 120 goals in 236 games. In his second (2006–07), he scored eight goals in 30. That is almost a goal every two games, up there with Mo Salah and Luis Suárez in the modern era.

Fowler made a good start, scoring on his 1993 debut in the League Cup in a 3–1 win at Fulham. Two weeks later, he astonished Anfield by scoring all five goals in a resounding second leg win. He was still only 18.

Robbie Fowler scored goals. The fans loved him so much, his nickname was God. He won three awards medals with Liverpool – an FA Cup, a League Cup and a UEFA Cup – but one award stands out as different: a certificate for Fair Play, from UEFA.

How did he win it?

It's 1996 and Liverpool are away at Arsenal. Robbie Fowler runs onto a long ball from his own defence. Somehow, every other player on the pitch has been cut out of the game and Fowler is one-on-one with David Seaman, the Arsenal keeper. One touch, then Seaman comes in at Fowler's feet, misses the ball and appears to touch Fowler's leg. But in slow motion, you can see Fowler leaps over Seaman's arm, then falling onto the pitch.

A penalty is given. But now Fowler is on his feet. He's insisting it's not a penalty. His arms are in the air.

'He didn't touch me,' Fowler would say in an interview years later. 'I jumped over him. I lost my balance. It's obviously not a penalty.'

In insisting he was not fouled, Fowler seemed to ensure that David Seaman was not sent off – even though the penalty stood. This in a time before VAR.

It was Robbie Fowler's duty to take the penalty. But when he hit it to the keeper's left, Seaman saved it. Sadly for Arsenal, the Liverpool forward, Jason McAteer, netted the rebound.

When asked if he had missed the penalty on

purpose, Fowler is quite clear: 'Not a chance.'

The UEFA Fair Play certificate hangs on the wall at Robbie Fowler's house. He says it has pride of place.

THE McMANAMAN FINAL

League Cup # 5

Sometimes a cup final is unofficially named after a player. There is the Gerrard final of 2005. Ten years before that, Liverpool won the 1995 League Cup – and there is no doubt as to which player's name would be forever attached to that triumph.

Another Liverpool legend: Steve McManaman.

His first goal epitomised all his qualities as a player. Running. Dribbling. Scoring goals.

McManaman received a pass from John Barnes close to the centre circle, turned with it and ran with the ball close to his feet towards the Bolton goal. Taking nine or ten touches and beating three or four players – it's hard to count exactly as his footwork is so intricate and dazzling – he found himself in the penalty area and poked the ball underneath the Bolton keeper.

One-nil on the 37th minute.

His second goal came after 68 minutes. Controlling a pass just inside the Bolton area he took the ball tight to the line, then worked his way into the Bolton penalty area. Nine or ten touches, using both feet to glide into the box and strike the ball low and hard again past the keeper.

Two-nil. The final was won. The McManaman final.

LIVERPOOL STOP MAN UNITED

Rivals

If you can't win the league yourselves, the next best thing is to stop your biggest rivals winning it. Liverpool achieved just that in 1992.

Manchester United had not been English Champions since 1967. Liverpool had won it 11 times in the meantime. Twenty-five years without being English Champions and Manchester United looked to be on target to end that quarter-century of pain and shame.

Until they came to Anfield.

The game ended 2–0 to Liverpool, prompting the commentator to call the season at that moment. 'The title goes to Leeds United. Without any doubt at all. Two-nil to Liverpool – it's all up for Manchester United."

The author of this book was at home that day,

sitting on his sofa, watching the match on the TV with his mum. A season ticket holder at Leeds since his childhood, he was 24 years old and he was in tears.

He will be forever grateful to Liverpool F.C.

RUSH TO VICTORY

FA Cup # 5

On paper, an FA Cup final between Liverpool and second-tier Sunderland looked like an easy win for the Reds. And it was an easy win. In the end.

But, for the majority of the first half, it was Sunderland who looked the most likely to score. Liverpool seemed nervy at the back, and Sunderland took advantage.

A desperate save from Bruce Grobbelaar who seemed to collide with the post as he scrambled to push a Sunderland shot away. A terrible miss from a Sunderland striker in acres of space, unmarked. A poor clearance from Jan Mølby that almost set up a Sunderland goal. Nervy moments.

At half time it could have been 3–0 to the team from the league below.

But Liverpool had forwards in abundance.

Ray Houghton. Michael Thomas. Ian Rush. Dean Saunders. Steve McManaman. Surely class would tell.

And it did.

In the second half Liverpool took control. Another dazzling dribble from Steve McManaman set up Michael Thomas to blast home from an angle.

One-nil.

Now Liverpool were all over the Wearsiders. A shot from Jan Mølby saved. A Dean Saunders strike bouncing back off the bar. Then Saunders with the ball again. With a pass to Michael Thomas, who touched it to Ian Rush in the penalty area.

Goal. Two-nil.

There was no coming back for Sunderland. Liverpool had won their fifth FA Cup.

DOMINATION

English Champions # 18

When Liverpool won the league in the 1989–90 season they became English Champions for the 18th time, by far the most titles at the time. Arsenal and Everton had nine each, only half as many as Liverpool had achieved. At that point in history Manchester United had won only seven league titles.

With players like Ian Rush and Peter Beardsley, Steve McMahon and John Aldridge tormenting defences, and with Alan Hansen and Bruce Grobbelaar keeping other teams out, no-one could compete and Liverpool finished nine points clear of their nearest challengers, Aston Villa.

With that success, Liverpool F.C. had dominated English football for almost two decades, having won it for 11 out of the previous 17 seasons.

Then, over the next two decades, something

changed and history shifted. By 2013 Manchester United would be on 20 titles, Liverpool still on 18.

The Liverpool F.C. website remarks on this strange period of history as well as anyone could:

'Few could have foreseen then that it would take another three decades for the Reds to resume their position at the summit of English football, when Klopp finally brought number 19 to Anfield.'

ENGLISH LEAGUE DIVISION ONE, 1989–90								
	P	W	D	L	F	A	GD	Pts
Liverpool	38	23	10	5	78	37	+41	79
Aston Villa	38	21	7	10	57	38	+19	70
Spurs	38	19	6	13	59	47	+12	63

THE MERSEYSIDE FINAL

FA Cup # 4

Just five weeks after the darkest day in the history of Liverpool F.C. – the Hillsborough disaster – Liverpool faced the other footballing giants of Merseyside, Everton, in the 1989 FA Cup final.

Before the game, Gerry Marsden of the group Gerry and the Pacemakers sang 'You'll Never Walk Alone' to the crowd. A deeply emotional moment and a song that means so much to the Liverpool faithful.

At the time Everton were also a successful club, having won the FA Cup and two league titles in the previous six years.

Just four minutes into the game, the Liverpool striker, John Aldridge, clipped a crisp shot into the back of the net. One-nil to the Reds. The lead lasted for almost the whole match, a full 86 minutes. Until, with the last kick of normal time, Stuart McCall equalised for Everton.

Liverpool fans felt a deep, deep frustration. They had been so close!

But Liverpool began extra time in the same way they began normal time, using the exciting array of attacking talent they had at the time. An early goal after five minutes. Ian Rush, on as a substitute, taking the ball on his chest, turning, then cracking the ball past his Wales international teammate in the Everton goal, Neville Southall.

Two-one to the Reds.

Then Everton came back at them again. Attack after attack until Stuart McCall scored for a second time.

Two-all.

But then – just two minutes after McCall's equaliser – John Barnes took the ball and curled in a perfect cross to dissect the Everton defence and find Ian Rush. Rush, knowing he had to head it perfectly to defeat Southall, angled his body and headed the ball into the ground, so that it bounced out of reach of the Everton keeper and into the goal.

Three-two to Liverpool. They had won their fourth FA Cup.

NO RUSH

English Champions # 17

Liverpool once again played the 1987–88 season without their talismanic striker, Ian Rush, who had moved to Juventus the season before.

Rush was a devastating finisher. Over his seven seasons at Anfield, he scored 109 goals in 182 appearances. The question still lingered whether the Reds could continue to challenge for the league without him.

Liverpool began that season with a then unbeaten record of 29 games.

So the answer was yes.

Rush had been replaced as part of a whole new attacking trio of John Aldridge, John Barnes and Peter Beardsley.

That trio ended the second season without Rush as the leading scorers at the club: Aldridge with 28 goals,

Beardsley 18 and Barnes 17.

And Liverpool were champions again – even without Ian Rush.

ENGLISH LEAGUE DIVISION ONE, 1987–88								
	P	W	D	L	F	A	GD	Pts
Liverpool	40	26	12	2	87	24	+63	90
Man United	40	23	12	3	71	38	+33	81
Nottm Forest	40	20	13	7	67	39	+28	73

LIVERPOOL 7 EVERTON 2

Super League Cup 1986

How did Liverpool become the only team to win the Screen Sport Super League Cup, probably the most obscure tournament in the history of the English game?

The idea for the Super League Cup was that it would give the English clubs that had been banned from the three European tournaments – the European Cup, the Cup Winners Cup and the UEFA Cup – a chance to play each other in a tournament to raise lost income. This was because of the English involvement in the Heysel Stadium disaster of May 1985, in which 39 people were killed.

The Super League Cup was played during the 1985–86 season, with a two-leg final at the beginning of the 1986–87 season.

Six teams qualified. The English champions

(Everton), the FA Cup winners (Manchester United), the League Cup winners (Norwich City) and the teams that would have qualified for the UEFA Cup had English teams not been banned (Liverpool, Tottenham and Southampton).

Liverpool overcame Tottenham and Southampton in a mini-league format, then beat Norwich in the semi-final.

The final was played over two legs between Liverpool and Everton. The Reds won 3–1 at Anfield and 4–1 at Goodison Park, so won by a 7–2 aggregate score.

Ian Rush netted five goals in that final.

The tournament, however, was never held again. Attendances for the games were low, and it didn't raise the money the organisers had hoped it would.

ALAN HANSEN

Player

Alan Hansen is one of the most decorated footballers in the history of Liverpool F.C. – meaning that he has won a lot of winners' medals.

Arguably his greatest moment, during a twelve-year career with the best team in England at the time, was being made captain when Kenny Dalglish took over as manager in 1985. Hansen led the team that achieved Liverpool's most successful domestic season, the only time the club has been Champions of England and FA Cup winners.

The double.

As captain, Alan Hansen lifted both trophies that season.

But his overall career stands out to make him one of the true Liverpool greats. His contribution to the success of Liverpool F.C. is immense.

TOM PALMER

Hansen joined Liverpool in 1977 and left in 1990. During that period, he was part of the team that won three of Liverpool's six European Cups, eight league titles, two FA Cups and four League Cups.

It was a time when Liverpool were expected to win most of the competitions they participated in – and that was very much down to players like Alan Hansen.

THE DOUBLE AT LAST

FA Cup # 3

If Liverpool F.C. had not existed, then May 1986 could have seen Everton win the English league and cup double for the only time in their history.

But disappointingly for Everton, Liverpool do exist.

Seven days after winning their 16th English Championship, and just two points ahead of their Merseyside neighbours, Liverpool faced Everton in the 1986 FA Cup final.

Clearly the two best teams in England competing for the world's most famous domestic football trophy.

At half time, it looked like that trophy might be on its way to Goodison, not Anfield. Everton led with a goal by Gary Lineker, scoring the fortieth goal of his season. An extraordinary total for a man who would be a household name a generation later as host of *Match of the Day*.

But Liverpool – as they have shown throughout their history – are not a team to give up in cup finals. Player-manager Kenny Dalglish must have talked a good game at half time because the second half of the final belonged to Liverpool.

After 56 minutes, the Danish international, Jan Mølby, slid the ball to Ian Rush in the penalty area. Rush touched the ball out of the reach of Everton keeper, Bobby Mimms and rolled the ball into the net. The scores were level.

Six minutes later, Mølby had the ball in the area once again. He slid a perfectly weighted cross to Craig Johnston, who buried the ball in the net.

Two-one.

Liverpool were ahead.

But the game was not over. For the next 20 minutes, roared on by the Everton faithful, the Blues did not give up. Then, with just seven minutes to go, Jan Mølby – the Dane in there again – played a tidy ball to Ronnie Whelan, who passed to Ian Rush. Rush, showing his trademark composure, controlled the ball and slotted it home.

LIVERPOOL'S GREATEST MOMENTS

Three-one. The FA Cup was going to Anfield, not Goodison.

And so Everton did not win the double.

Liverpool did and they joined Arsenal and Tottenham as the only teams to achieve that since the beginning of the twentieth century. For now.

PLAYER, MANAGER, LEGEND

Champions # 16

When Joe Fagan retired as Liverpool manager in May 1985, Kenny Dalglish took over as player manager. Dalglish was only 34 years old and extremely young for a manager. With Everton and Manchester United so strong at the time, there were doubts that Liverpool could compete for the league.

Two months into the 1985–86 season Manchester United were top with 10 wins out of 10, chasing their first league championship since 1967. It seemed those doubts about Liverpool were correct.

But Manchester United faltered and – during the winter months – Everton were relentless, taking over at the top of the league. As champions the season before, Everton were everyone's favourites to win it again. By late February – two thirds of the way through the season – Everton were 10 points clear of

Liverpool. After winning at Anfield on 22 February – the Toffeemen were a massive 13 points ahead.

But then Liverpool went on a run – a quite astonishing run of results that crushed Everton and Manchester United's hopes. Over the final 12 games Liverpool won eleven and drew one. They scored 32 goals and conceded only 4.

The last game of the season was away at Chelsea. Liverpool needed to win to be sure to stay above Everton and win the title.

There was one goal in the game. Liverpool worked the ball up field, Jim Beglin lofted the ball into the penalty area and Kenny Dalglish was in – at speed – to take the ball on his chest, then volley it into the Chelsea net.

At the end of Dalglish's first full season as manager, Liverpool were champions.

TOM PALMER

ENGLISH LEAGUE DIVISION ONE, 1985–86								
	P	W	D	L	F	A	GD	Pts
Liverpool	42	26	10	6	89	37	+52	88
Everton	42	26	8	8	87	41	+46	86
West Ham	42	26	6	10	74	40	+34	84

THE FOURTH

European Cup # 4

The 1984 European Cup final – Liverpool v Roma – will always be associated with the Zimbabwean goalkeeper Bruce Grobbelaar, and how his wobbly legs routine earned him the nickname the Clown.

The pressure was all on Liverpool. Roma were familiar with the pitch, the stadium and had more fans in the ground. It wasn't entirely fair. But that didn't matter. Not in the end.

Phil Neal opened the scoring on 13 minutes with a bizarre goal. The Roma keeper, Tancredi, leapt for the ball, lost it and fell on the pitch. As he was trying to get back onto his feet and grab the ball, one of his defenders tried to hoof the ball away, only hitting it hard against Tancredi's head, the ball ricocheting to Neal between two defenders. Neal, calm amid the chaos, slotted it home.

One-nil to Liverpool.

But Pruzzo equalised before half time with a deft header and the game ended level after extra time.

And so to penalties.

Steve Nicol missed the first for Liverpool, but with Phil Neal, Graeme Souness and Ian Rush scoring their spot kicks and Antonio Conti missing, it was 3–3 with one penalty left for each team.

Roma's Graziani came forward to take his. But – as he lined up the ball – Bruce Grobbelaar performed a weird dance on the goal-line, his legs wobbling from side to side. The Italian tried to focus, but his fierce shot hit the bar. Roma had missed. Liverpool needed only to score and they would be winners.

Did Bruce Grobbelaar's antics put the Italian off? The Liverpool keeper would be known as the Clown by the Roma players, so maybe.

Either way, Alan Kennedy hammered in the last penalty and Liverpool were Champions of Europe for the fourth time. And Joe Fagan had won the League Cup and the English and European Championships in his first season as boss.

SOUNESS POWER

League Cup # 4

The 1984 League Cup final was played between the two dominant English teams of the era: Liverpool and their neighbours, Everton. Liverpool had won the previous three League Cup finals, whereas Everton had never won it.

The game was played over two games, with the first, at Wembley, ending in a goalless draw.

There were several standout moments. They included a powerful long-range shot from Graeme Souness that Neville Southall managed to cling onto and keep the scores level. And a clear handball from Liverpool defender, Alan Hansen, stopping a certain goal.

Everton fans were furious. But the referee did not see it. Nor did the linesman. And VAR was not going to exist for another few decades. So the game went to a replay, three days later, at Manchester City's old stadium, Maine Road. And the Everton fans had to hope that they would be able to avenge the injustice of Wembley.

The replay was just as tight. Both teams showed that Merseyside dominated the English game – but there would be no revenge for the Everton fans.

This was because the one goal of the replay was scored on 21 minutes by the Liverpool captain. Graeme Souness, perhaps frustrated that his long-range shot had not beaten Neville Southall in the Everton goal in the previous match, took a pass from Phil Neal with his back to goal. He clipped the ball up, turned, and then – using his famously powerful shot – blasted it past the Everton keeper.

One-nil to Liverpool.

It would be the only goal in 210 minutes of football. But it would be enough to win Liverpool their fourth League Cup on the trot.

THE GREATEST?

Champions # 15

The Liverpool team that won the 1983–84 English Championship is considered one of the greatest teams to grace the English game. Just looking at the team sheet of those who played the most time is like looking at a hall of fame:

Bruce Grobbelaar in goal. A back four of Phil Neal, Alan Kennedy, Mark Lawrenson and Alan Hansen. A midfield of Graeme Souness, Sammy Lee, Michael Robinson and Craig Johnston. Then Ian Rush and Kenny Dalglish up front.

With only 6 defeats out of 42 games and with Ian Rush scoring 47 goals in 65 games, Liverpool stormed the league. They had already won the League Cup. And having become League Champions, they would now go on to their fourth European Cup Final and the chance of a historic and unprecedented treble for the manager who had been worried he would end his first season with nothing.

ENGLISH LEAGUE DIVISION ONE, 1983–84								
	P	W	D	L	F	A	GD	Pts
Liverpool	42	22	14	6	73	32	+51	80
Southampton	42	22	11	9	66	38	+28	77
Nottm Forest	42	22	8	12	76	45	+31	74

BOB PAISLEY LIFTS HIS FINAL CUP

League Cup # 3

The 1983 League Cup Final – known as the Milk Cup back then – will be remembered for three exceptional goals, but even more for who lifted the trophy.

It's an honour normally reserved for the captain of the winning team – but today would be different.

But first… the goals.

Goal one came from Manchester United's 17-year-old Norman Whiteside. Taking the ball with his back to goal, he skinned Alan Hansen and fired the ball past Bruce Grobbelaar. United were 1–0 ahead, with only 12 minutes played.

After 75 minutes, Alan Kennedy shot from 30 yards, beating the despairing dive of Manchester's goalkeeper, Gary Bailey. Then, eight minutes into extra time, Ronnie Whelan struck, the ball coming back to him off a Manchester United defender, giving him the chance to curl a beautiful shot into the top corner.

Two-one to Liverpool. And that was it.

But the actual greatest moment of the day came after Liverpool had won their third League Cup.

It was the last trophy won by legendary manager, Bob Paisley. In his nine seasons as manager, he had led the team to win 15 major honours, including three European and six English championships. The most successful period in the history of Liverpool F.C.

And so, after the game, the Liverpool players insisted that their manager should collect the trophy. The football world watched and applauded as Bob Paisley climbed the steps, a Liverpool scarf draped round his neck, to lift the League Cup.

ENGLISH CHAMPIONS # 14

League

Liverpool's 14th English championship win in 1983 was Bob Paisley's last. On his retirement, Paisley was the club's most successful manager with six league championships and three European Cups, retired.

The Reds started strongly, creating a huge lead until April. After 35 games their record looked like this: won 24, drawn 8, lost 3.

And even though Liverpool lost five and drew two of their last games, collecting only two more points, they had done enough, winning the league by 11 points.

ENGLISH LEAGUE DIVISION ONE, 1982–83								
	P	W	D	L	F	A	GD	Pts
Liverpool	42	24	10	8	87	37	+50	82
Watford	42	22	5	15	74	57	+17	71
Man United	42	19	13	19	56	38	+28	70

Paisley had done it again. But that era was over now. Paisley was retiring.

Other clubs in the league would have been relieved to see the back of him. When a winner leaves a club, it gives the other teams a chance to win. Would Joe Fagan and Kenny Dalglish, the club's next two managers, be able to keep Liverpool at the top of the English game?

History tells us yes.

Bob Paisley had joined Liverpool in 1939 as a player and stayed very involved with the club after 1983, acting as an advisor to Fagan and Dalglish. After that he became a club director. He finally retired in 1992, completing over half a century's involvement with Liverpool F.C.

PRESENT V PAST

League Cup # 2

Liverpool's second league cup win came against Tottenham Hotspur in March 1982 with a familiar face in goal.

The club's most recent final before that day – the defeat of Real Madrid in the European Cup final of 1981 – featured Ray Clemence, the club's most successful goalkeeper with five league championships, two domestic cup and five European trophies.

Yet now, in the 1982 league cup, Clemence would be in goal for the opposition, having been sold to Tottenham in the previous summer, and replaced with Bruce Grobbelaar.

It must have been strange for the Liverpool scorers, Ronnie Whelan with two and Ian Rush with one, to put the ball past such a Liverpool legend.

Spurs took the lead in the eleventh minute but in

typical Liverpool cup final fashion, their opponents did not give up. They kept on at Spurs until the 87th minute, when Whelan took a cross from the right and slotted the ball home.

The winning goal – scored well into the second half of extra time – was the best. Ian Rush picked up a poor pass and played Kenny Dalglish into the penalty area in plenty of space. Dalglish took one touch, then appeared to dance lightly on both feet for several seconds, bamboozling the defender, before playing a neat pass to Ronnie Whelan who smashed the ball over the exposed Ray Clemence.

LEGACY SHANKLY

Champions # 12

The 1981–82 football season was the first to award three points for a win in England. The idea came from Jimmy Hill, then host of *Match of the Day*, and it was trialled in England before being adopted across the world.

But the first half of that season was very difficult for Liverpool F.C. – in more ways than one.

By Christmas, the club were mid-table, having won only 6 out of their 17 games.

But far more significantly, also that December, Bill Shankly – the manager who began generations of success at Liverpool – had died.

As 1981 became 1982 Liverpool had 16 games left. With 48 points under the new system to play for, Liverpool won 42 of them, winning 13 matches and drawing the other three. They lost none of their games. It was a breathtaking run.

On the last Saturday of the season Liverpool had to avoid defeat against Tottenham at home. They won. Three-one.

Liverpool were champions of England for the 12th time.

Life without Bill Shankly had to go on and did go on. With more success. But the club's latest championship was an achievement that would not have been possible without the foundations built by the great man.

ENGLISH LEAGUE DIVISION ONE, 1981–82								
	P	W	D	L	F	A	GD	Pts
Liverpool	42	26	9	7	80	32	+48	87
Ipswich	42	26	5	11	75	53	+22	83
Man United	42	22	12	8	59	29	+30	78

HANSEN HEADS HOME

League Cup # 1

Liverpool's first League Cup win in 1981 came after 20 failed attempts. And to win it they needed two games – against West Ham United.

The first game at Wembley ended in a draw. With no goals scored in the first half, second half or even the first half of extra time, each team scored once in the last three minutes of extra time. A replay was needed.

During the replay, three goals came in the first half hour. West Ham opened the scoring, but then a skilful volley from Kenny Dalglish and a bullet header from Alan Hansen meant Liverpool could take the lead on 28 minutes.

The rest of the game played out with no more goals. And Liverpool had won the League Cup for the first time. Since then, they have won the trophy 10 times in 45 seasons.

THE THIRD

European Champions # 3

Alan and Ray Kennedy were not brothers, but the way they co-operated at a throw-in to score the winning goal at the 1981 European Cup Final, they could have been. Or was it just that the whole Liverpool team had such an understanding of each other it seemed like telepathy?

Liverpool were playing Real Madrid, the true giants of the European game. Real had been champions of Europe six times, while Liverpool had triumphed twice.

It was a tight game with both sides testing the goalkeepers, but only from a distance. Real's defence was well organised, hard to get behind and long-range shots on target from Alan Kennedy, Kenny Dalglish and Terry McDermott failed to break the deadlock.

Eighty-one minutes in, the score remained 0–0. The game was heading for extra time.

Until that throw-in.

Spotting Alan Kennedy on the edge of the area, Ray Kennedy threw the ball to him. Alan chested the ball into the penalty area, and let it drop and bounce on between two defenders. Somehow Ray's throw and Alan's chest-control had broken the mean Spanish defence open and now Alan was in space, with just the keeper to beat. He hit it.

Goal. One-nil!

Liverpool had joined Real Madrid, Bayern and Ajax in the select group of teams who had won three or more European Cups.

And Bob Paisley became the first manager in history to win it three times.

LAST DAY GLORY

English champions # 12

Throughout the 1979–80 season, there was an intense tussle between Liverpool and Manchester United.

The rivals would head into the last month of the season as the only two that could realistically win the title. The tension was ratcheted up on 5 April when Liverpool travelled to Old Trafford and were beaten 2–1.

Could Manchester United do what they had not done since 1967 and beat Liverpool to the league?

It was a possibility.

But this Liverpool team had the likes of Ray Clemence, Ray Kennedy, Graeme Souness, Kenny Dalglish and the two Phils: Thompson and Neal, all playing 40 or more games in the league alone. That's seven players playing almost every game in one season.

After Manchester United won against them,

LIVERPOOL'S GREATEST MOMENTS

Liverpool were just two points ahead of them in the league table. With two points counting for a win, Liverpool had to avoid a very heavy defeat to Aston Villa to be sure of being crowned champions again.

But Liverpool managed to dodge that disaster very easily – by winning 4–1. And, with Manchester United losing 2–0 at Leeds United (Leeds being cheered on in the stadium by this author, age 12, as a matter of fact), Liverpool were champions for the twelfth time.

David Johnson's two goals that day against Villa made him leading scorer for Liverpool that season, with 22 in the league and 27 in total.

ENGLISH LEAGUE DIVISION ONE, 1978–79								
	P	W	D	L	F	A	GD	Pts
Liverpool	42	25	10	7	81	30	+51	60
Man United	42	24	10	8	65	35	+30	58

WE WANT PAISLEY

English champions # 11

For their eleventh league title in 1978–79, Liverpool's team was clearly one of the greatest that had graced the English game.

With Ray Clemence, Phil Neal and Alan Kennedy not missing a league game all season, and with Kenny Dalglish and Graeme Souness missing only one, you can see why they were so good.

Other names that helped make that season so remarkable were Alan Hansen, Phil Thompson, Jimmy Case, Sammy Lee, Emlyn Hughes, and Terry McDermott.

And the manager, of course: Bob Paisley. Quiet, unassuming, happy for his players to take the limelight.

But it's not just these names that tell the story of that season – what of Liverpool's numbers and statistics?

A record number of points in the English top flight: 68.

An average of more than two goals scored per game: 85 goals in 42 games.

Only 16 goals conceded in 42 games, and just four conceded in 21 home games. In league games alone, Ray Clemence, the Liverpool keeper, kept 28 clean sheets.

In other words: the stats reflect Liverpool's league domination as much as the names of the players.

But the last word that season came from the fans. After beating Aston Villa 3–0 at Anfield, and winning the league, the Liverpool players did a lap of honour and finally left 50,000 fans celebrating on the terraces to celebrate their achievement back in the dressing room.

But a chanting noise from the fans outside, growing louder and louder, could not be ignored in that dressing room.

'We want Paisley! We want Paisley!'

The story goes that the players insisted Bob Paisley go out to acknowledge the fans. He agreed. He walked

20 yards out onto the pitch, waved to the fans, then retreated again.

Because Bob Paisley didn't want the glory for himself: he wanted to bring glory to Liverpool F.C.

ENGLISH LEAGUE DIVISION ONE, 1978–79								
	P	W	D	L	F	A	GD	Pts
Liverpool	42	30	8	4	85	16	+69	68
Nottm Forest	42	21	18	3	61	26	+35	60

IAN CALLAGHAN

Player

Ian Callaghan is the player who played the most games for Liverpool F.C. It is unlikely his record will ever be beaten.

He played 857 times for the Reds.

His career was remarkable not just for its longevity, but for its journey. He joined the club when Liverpool were last in the English second division (now known as the Championship). By the time he left, Liverpool had won the European Cup – twice. If you were to tell that story through the career of just one player, it would have to be through Ian Callaghan, the only one who lasted the whole journey.

A midfielder, Callaghan could not have imagined such success for himself and his club when he was given his debut in 1960 by Liverpool's new manager of the time, Bill Shankly. In 1962, Liverpool were promoted to the top flight and have remained there ever since.

Callaghan played his 857 Liverpool games in all competitions, winning five English Championships, two FA Cups, two UEFA cups, two European Cups and one European Super Cup.

In 1974 he became the first Liverpool player to win the Football Writers' Association player of the year. The following year he received an MBE.

Ian Callaghan had people's respect – in the game and out of it.

THE SECOND

European Cup # 2

After winning Liverpool's first European Cup in 1977, the captain, Emlyn Hughes, was asked: 'Well, what are you going to do now?'

He replied, 'All we can do is win it again.'

So that is exactly what they did.

Liverpool's second European Cup final took place at Wembley in 1978, giving them the advantage of knowing the venue well – they had appeared in five finals there over the previous few years.

Even so, if you look at a map of Europe, Club Brugge, their Belgian opponents, is located closer to Wembley than Anfield. As the crow flies.

The Belgians played it tight, a defensive style that frustrated Liverpool and led to long-range shots from Jimmy Case and Graeme Souness testing the goalkeeper, along with a header from Alan Hansen.

But the Reds could not find a way through.

Until the 64th minute.

It was a beautiful goal. After yet another Liverpool attack, the ball came out of the area to Graeme Souness. The Scotsman chested it down, then played a sweet pass through three Belgian defenders to another Scottish international, Kenny Dalglish.

Unmarked, Dalglish waited for the ball to come to him and for the keeper to commit to a low save with his legs – and then, in the crucial split second, Dalglish lofted a shot over the keeper and into the goal.

Liverpool 1 Club Brugge 0. And that was how it finished. Emlyn Hughes had done exactly what he had suggested. Liverpool had won the European Cup. Again.

AFTER KEEGAN

Super Cup # 1

The European Super Cup trophy came into being in 1973 as a game between the winners of the two foremost European trophies: the European Cup (now known as the Champions League) and the European Cup Winners Cup (now defunct).

In 1977, Liverpool won the Super Cup for the first and only time in the 20th century – and it came with a twist. They lined up against the German team, Hamburger SV, a team made up mostly of German players and one English player.

Kevin Keegan.

Keegan had been a legend at Liverpool from 1971 before leaving in 1977 for half a million pounds, a British transfer record at that point. Keegan had been Liverpool's leading scorer during the previous season, with 20 goals.

The final was played over two legs. A 1–1 draw in Germany was cancelled out by a thumping 6–0 win for Liverpool at Anfield, with Terry McDermott scoring a hat-trick for Liverpool. McDermott would become an increasingly prolific goal scorer after Keegan's departure from Merseyside; in 1980–81 he would be Liverpool's leading goal scorer with 22.

Liverpool would win the Super Cup three more times: in 2001, 2005 and 2019. Only Real Madrid, Barcelona and AC Milan have won it more often.

HOWARD GAYLE

Player

Howard Gayle was the first Black footballer to play for Liverpool F.C.

He joined the club as a full professional in 1977, having come through the Liverpool youth team. He was a local lad, having been born and brought up in Toxteth, and he was proud to be so.

Gayle, a forward, played four times for the club in an era when he was up against a generation of exceptional talent.

His most important appearance was in the semi-final of the 1980–81 European Cup at Bayern Munich. Liverpool had to avoid defeat to go through to the final. When Kenny Dalglish came off injured in the ninth minute, Gayle came on and played with exceptional maturity to help Liverpool see the game through, against 70,000 hostile German fans and opposition players who fouled him repeatedly.

Gayle was on the bench for the victorious European Cup Final of 1981.

As well as earning a European Cup final medal, he was a member of the England U21 team that won the 1984 UEFA Championship.

After his footballing career Gayle said: 'It was constantly in the press that I was the first Black player to play for Liverpool. It was a landmark as far as Black people were concerned, and I was proud to represent the Black community of Liverpool.'

Howard Gayle would go on to be an inspiration to the next generation of Black footballers in the city. There is a mural in the city to mark his achievements.

KENNY DALGLISH

First season

The name Kenny Dalglish has come up in this book again and again – as a manager of a side that won multiple titles and trophies, and as a player who did the same.

He arrived at Anfield in 1977 when he was signed from Celtic F.C., one of the two big teams from his home city of Glasgow. He was bought to replace Kevin Keegan, who had signed for Hamburg in Germany.

Kevin Keegan's boots were huge ones to fill. He was a Liverpool legend, and all eyes would be scrutinising how the 26-year-old Scot, Dalglish, would cope with his first season with the reigning European Champions. Many players fail when given this sort of a challenge.

This is how Kenny Dalglish's first season played out: He scored on his league debut away to

Middlesbrough – after seven minutes.

He scored on his Anfield debut – the opening goal in a 2–0 defeat of Newcastle.

He scored in his first cup game, a 2–0 defeat of Chelsea.

He scored in six of his first seven league and cup games for the club.

At the end of the 1977–78 season – his first at the club – he had scored 31 goals in 62 games. That's one goal every two games.

His last goal of his first season was the winner in the 1978 European Cup final.

Kenny Dalglish was extraordinary.

And that was just his first season.

THE FIRST

European Cup 1977

Liverpool kicked off the 1977 European Cup final against Borussia Mönchengladbach, hoping to be the third British team to be crowned champions of Europe, following 1967 winners Celtic and Manchester United in 1968.

It was a particularly big day for Tommy Smith, playing his 600th game for Liverpool. Born in the city and a fan of the club, Smith had been signed as a schoolboy, making his first team debut 14 years before, in April 1963. He was a key part of the generation of footballers that made Liverpool one of the biggest teams in the world.

Liverpool scored first. After nearly half an hour, Ian Callaghan won the ball in midfield, advanced, then passed to Steve Heighway, who touched a perfect ball to Terry McDermott in the penalty area.

One-nil.

Mönchengladbach equalised after half time. But Liverpool believed. They pressed. And on 65 minutes they won a corner. Steve Heighway went over to take it and hit a perfect corner to Tommy Smith, who headed it powerfully home.

Two-one.

Two superb assists from Steve Heighway. But all the focus had to be on the goal scorer. On his 600th appearance.

'It's Tommy Smith,' the commentator sang. 'Oh… what an end to a career!'

Phil Neal added a third goal from a penalty and Liverpool were champions of Europe for the first time.

The first time of six.

TWICE CHAMPIONS

English Champions # 10

Liverpool's 1976–77 English league championship was won under great pressure as the team fought to win an unprecedented treble of league title, FA Cup and European Cup.

In an era of small squads where 15 players played 28 or more games in the league, leaving three players in single figures, a huge amount of pressure was put on a few men, week after week.

As the season came to an end – with Liverpool playing cup quarter and semi-finals – their league form faltered, with the team drawing three and losing one of their last four games.

But they did enough to become crowned league champions for the 10th time, finishing just one point ahead of Manchester City.

Liverpool went on to lose the FA Cup final to

Manchester United that season, but won their first European Cup. Even with that Wembley defeat, Liverpool delivered their best season's performance to date.

Champions of England. Champions of Europe.

ENGLISH LEAGUE DIVISION ONE, 1976–77								
	P	W	D	L	F	A	GD	Pts
Liverpool	42	23	11	8	62	33	+29	57
Man City	42	21	14	7	60	34	+26	56
Ipswich	42	22	8	12	66	39	+25	52

TEN DAY WAIT

League Champions # 9

There was one game left in the 1975–76 season. With most of the final fixtures played on 25 April 1976, the league table stood like this:

ENGLISH LEAGUE DIVISION ONE, 1975–76								
	P	W	D	L	F	A	GD	Pts
QPR	42	24	11	7	67	33	+34	59
Liverpool	41	22	14	5	63	30	+33	58

Liverpool and Queens Park Rangers (QPR) had been neck and neck for weeks. It was tight. It was tense. It was turbulent.

The final game. Wolves v Liverpool on 4 May. Like a cup final, really, with Liverpool needing a win to be sure of being crowned champions for the ninth time.

With 15 minutes remaining of the final game of the season, Liverpool were losing 1–0 and it looked like QPR would be champions. Then on 76 minutes, Kevin Keegan equalised. There was hope.

Five minutes left and John Toshack scored for Liverpool again. Two-one. The Reds just had to hold on for five more minutes.

And then – a minute later – another goal. For Liverpool again. Ray Kennedy. Three-one.

The season was over. The league table looked like this:

ENGLISH LEAGUE DIVISION ONE, 1975–76								
	P	W	D	L	F	A	GD	Pts
Liverpool	42	23	14	5	66	31	+35	60
QPR	42	24	11	7	67	33	+34	59

For the ninth time, Liverpool were champions of England.

COMEBACK KINGS

UEFA Cup # 2

Fifteen minutes into the first leg of the UEFA Cup final in April 1976 and Liverpool were 2–0 down at Anfield. Unthinkable.

And Club Brugge were not done. They were attacking again and again, intent on scoring more. Liverpool did well to keep the score at 2–0 by half time.

Bob Paisley – hoping to win his first trophy as manager after replacing the legendary Bill Shankly – had to do something. Change things. Find a way back into the final. His team talk that night, his tactical changes and a substitution changed everything.

If you watch the footage, you can see how the Liverpool Number 5 – Ray Kennedy – was the source of three goals scored on 59, 61 and 65 minutes.

An extraordinary passage of play that demolished the Belgians:

Firstly, a powerful shot from Ray Kennedy himself.

Then, another shot from Kennedy that came off the post, allowing Jimmy Case to bury the rebound.

Finally, Kennedy again, playing Steve Heighway in to run into the penalty area and be chopped down, before Keegan scored the penalty.

In just six minutes the score had gone from 0–2 to 3–2. A breathtaking comeback by Liverpool.

Now on to Belgium for the second leg. The Reds with a slender lead.

Liverpool must have been suffering flashbacks when, at Belgium's Olympiastadion, Brugge took a 1–0 lead, equalising on aggregate after 11 minutes. The goal came out of a penalty converted after a Tommy Smith handball.

What now? Would Liverpool crumble again?

No. They would not.

Because Liverpool F.C. were a team – a club, even – learning how to win trophies. Instead of defending deep, and panicking, Liverpool fought back and four minutes later, in this second leg, Kevin Keegan equalised.

Now, after fifteen minutes, Liverpool led 4–3 on aggregate. That was how the score stayed, and that was how Liverpool won the 1976 UEFA Cup.

BOB PAISLEY TAKES OVER

Foundations

In 1999 a new gateway was unveiled in front of the Kop End at Anfield. Called the Paisley Gateway, it remembers the most successful manager in the history of Liverpool F.C.

Back in 1975 Liverpool's legendary Bill Shankly unexpectedly announced his retirement as manager. Bob Paisley, a member of Shankly's coaching team, was offered the job of replacing him and eventually accepted.

But Paisley only took the job after trying to persuade Shankly to stay on. Paisley would have preferred to work under Shankly. But it was not to be and the man from County Durham became Shankly's successor.

In his nine seasons in charge at Anfield, Paisley won six league championships, three European Cups, two UEFA cups and three league cups.

Unmatched before his time. And probably unmatchable in the future.

TALKING ON THE PITCH

FA Cup #2

Before the 1974 FA Cup final, the Newcastle striker, Malcolm Macdonald created extra tension by claiming that he was going to destroy Liverpool and win Newcastle's first domestic cup since 1955.

You don't really see it on the short highlights of the game on YouTube, but on that day, a 20-year-old Phil Thompson, in his first season as a regular first-team player for Liverpool, marked the noisy Newcastle star out of the game.

Liverpool won 3–0. They did their talking on the pitch. And their clean sheet was very much thanks to Thompson and Liverpool's defence.

The goals came from Kevin Keegan. His first, on 57 minutes, was a beauty – Keegan receiving a pass on the edge of the area by chipping it up in front of him, then volleying it through the fingers of the Newcastle keeper. His second, on 88 minutes, was a tap in from a Tommy Smith cross. Steve Heighway scored the other goal in the 3–0 rout.

Phil Thompson would go on to win 17 major honours with Liverpool over his 12 seasons. Meanwhile, Macdonald would never win a major trophy.

Two players from that day's Newcastle team would, however, go on to win a lot of honours. Terry McDermott and Alan Kennedy both signed for Liverpool in subsequent years and became key players in the club's history.

TOSHACK... KEEGAN... GOAL

UEFA Cup # 1

The first of Liverpool's European trophies came in May 1973: a two-legged UEFA Cup final against Borussia Mönchengladbach of West Germany.

Before Germany was reunified in 1990, teams like both the Borussias: Dortmund and Mönchengladbach, as well as Bayern Munich, represented West Germany in football matches.

The UEFA Cup final was played over two legs in those days. Liverpool won the first leg at Anfield 3–0. The first two goals were classic early 1970s Liverpool – a high ball for the powerful Liverpool striker John Toshack to head down for Keegan to head or shoot home. Larry Lloyd scored Liverpool's third.

So Liverpool took a 3–0 advantage – a clear lead – into the second leg.

But at half time in the second leg the aggregate

score was 3–2, the West Germans scoring through Jupp Heynckes. Now Liverpool had to dig in and defend. Would they lose to the Germans again and come away without a European trophy? Again?

No.

With Ray Clemence in goal and Tommy Smith marshalling the defence, Liverpool held out and the first of their European trophies was won.

HOME FORM

English champions # 8

The 1972–73 league title was won by Liverpool thanks to a remarkable run of home results.

Over the season their home record was: won 17 (they won only 8 away); drew 3 (they drew 7 away); lost 1 (they lost 6 away).

That home form included the end of a run of 21 consecutive home wins – an astonishing achievement that beat all such records.

If you needed a fortress to win a war, Anfield was that fortress.

LIVERPOOL'S GREATEST MOMENTS

ENGLISH LEAGUE DIVISION ONE, 1972-73								
	P	W	D	L	F	A	GD	Pts
Liverpool	42	25	10	7	72	42	+30	60
Arsenal	42	23	11	8	57	43	+24	57
Leeds	42	21	11	10	71	45	+26	53

The next team to match and beat their achievement, by winning 22 matches at home on the trot, did not do so until 2020, nearly half a century later.

And that team would be Jürgen Klopp's Liverpool F.C. – on their way to winning the club's 19th English Championship.

YOU'LL NEVER WALK ALONE

Song

When you walk to Anfield Football Stadium you might pass the large wrought iron gates and see the words 'You'll Never Walk Alone'.

If you look on the tops of the countless Liverpool fans' badges, you'll see the words 'Liverpool Football Club Est 1892', then along the top of the badge the words 'You'll Never Walk Alone'.

And then, before kick-off, you'll hear tens of thousands of Liverpool fans singing the same song with a passion that will send shivers down your spine.

'You'll Never Walk Alone' is a club song quite unlike any other. Originally from a 1945 musical called *Carousel* it was later, in 1967, also recorded by Elvis Presley.

But it was the Liverpool band Gerry and the Pacemakers who made it the Liverpool F.C. anthem after they released a cover version of the song in 1963, which became a British number one hit single.

Bill Shankly was given the single – then on a seven-inch vinyl record – by the group's lead singer, Gerry Marsden. Shankly liked it. Its lyrics spoke to him of what Liverpool F.C. were all about.

And the rest is history.

THE HUNT FOR GLORY

League Champions # 7

Liverpool were the champions of England during the only year that England would win the World Cup.

1966.

Liverpool did it with 14 players – nine of them playing in all but one or two of the games. Ever presents were Ian Callaghan, Gerry Byrne and Tommy Lawrence, Tommy Smith and Ron Yeats. It is amazing to think that teams played with such small squads when clubs now have three times as many players in the top flight.

Roger Hunt ended up as leading scorer for both the club and the league, with 29 goals in 37 appearances.

Hunt was an extraordinary marksman, rivalling the likes of Mo Salah and Kenny Dalglish in the club's history. He played 404 times for Liverpool, scoring

244 goals, while his strike rate for England was 18 goals in 34 games.

His role for Liverpool that season was immense, but for England he also scored three goals in their six games of the World Cup finals, an enormous contribution to his country winning the trophy for the first and only time.

The successful Hunt for glory in 1966 was partly down to Roger.

ENGLISH LEAGUE DIVISION ONE, 1965–66								
	P	W	D	L	F	A	GD	Pts
Liverpool	42	26	9	7	79	34	+45	61
Leeds	42	23	9	10	79	38	+41	55
Burnley	42	24	7	11	79	47	+32	55

THE FINAL OF STORIES

FA Cup # 1

The 1965 FA Cup final was a final of stories.

The first story was that it was Liverpool's first FA Cup win. Astonishing for a team that had existed for 73 years and had already been champions of England six times. They had lost finals in 1914 (to Burnley) and 1950 (to Arsenal).

But perhaps it was third time lucky.

The second story concerned the heroics of Liverpool defender, Gerry Byrne, who broke his collarbone in the fifth minute and played on throughout the whole game (120 minutes, including extra time), even setting up Roger Hunt with Liverpool's opening goal.

Apparently, the Liverpool manager, Bill Shankly, didn't tell him the full extent of his injury until after the game. This was a time before substitutes, so Liverpool would have been down to 10 men.

The third story was that Leeds were fielding a footballer called Albert Johanneson. Johanneson was from South Africa and was the first Black footballer to play in an FA Cup final. It would be 13 more years before a Black player (Viv Anderson) represented England at Wembley.

In the dying moments of extra time in such a tight game, Ian St John's winning goal for Liverpool was enough to overcome a Leeds team who had only been promoted to the top flight that season.

Liverpool had won their first FA Cup. In fact, their first knockout competition win of all.

More would follow. Many more.

MATCH OF THE DAY # 1

1964

Liverpool F.C. made history when – on 22 August 1964 – they were the first team to be the host stadium for BBC TV's *Match of the Day*.

It was the first day of the 1963–64 season, and Liverpool were hosting Arsenal at Anfield.

In the 11th minute, the first goal ever seen on *Match of the Day* was scored by Liverpool goal machine, Roger Hunt.

The game ended 3–2 to Liverpool, so Liverpool were the first team to win a game televised on *Match of the Day*.

A moment of football history.

THE KIT

Liverpool did not play in a full red kit until 1964. Although they had played in a red top since 1896, it took decades for them to turn out in red tops, shorts and socks.

It was Bill Shankly's idea. Shankly was a revolutionary. Changing the club's training and fitness techniques, changing the style of play and changing all the details he felt might make Liverpool F.C. more successful.

On 25 November 1964, 72 years after they were founded, Liverpool ran out onto the pitch in an all-red kit.

Shankly is said to have believed that red spelled danger and suggested power. And also that his players looked 10 feet tall in red kits against the pitch and whatever colour their opponents were wearing.

Was Shankly right to think playing in a full red kit would bring Liverpool F.C. more success?

Either way, if you ask anyone which football team is most associated with the colour and nickname – the Reds – it is Liverpool. Man United fans might disagree, but to most they are known as the Red Devils… or go by other names.

GET USED TO THIS

League Champions # 6

Around the time Bill Shankly's Liverpool were promoted from the Second Division of 1961–62, the teams at the top of the First Division included Everton and Manchester United. Both huge rivals of the Reds – and of each other.

Bill Shankly said, after Liverpool finished eighth in 1962–63, their first season back in the First Division, that he had felt he almost had the squad to challenge for the championship. Fans of longer-established teams like Everton and Manchester United laughed at him.

For 1963–64, Shankly signed just one player to enhance his squad: Peter Thompson from Preston for £37,000.

Thompson would be an ever present that season and Liverpool – thanks to a run of six consecutive wins – would need to beat Arsenal in their last home game of the season.

They did so. Five-nil.

And so, with 31 goals from Roger Hunt and 21 from Ian St John, Liverpool were 1963–64 league champions with an extraordinary 92 goals scored between them.

ENGLISH LEAGUE DIVISION ONE, 1963–64								
	P	W	D	L	F	A	GD	Pts
Liverpool	42	26	5	11	92	45	+47	57
Man United	42	23	7	12	90	62	+38	53
Everton	42	21	10	11	84	64	+20	52

The two teams directly below them would have to get used to finishing below Liverpool. Because this league title would be the first of 13 Liverpool wins over the next 26 years. In that period Liverpool would win half the English league championships, their closest rivals being Everton (three titles) and several teams with two, including Manchester United.

RON YEATS

Player

When Bill Shankly signed Ron Yeats from Dundee United in 1961 for £20,000, he immediately made him captain of the team.

Shankly later said that the signing of Yeats was the turning point. The moment when the future of Liverpool F.C. would change. For the better.

Did it play out as Bill Shankly imagined?

It did.

In his first season, Yeats would lead Liverpool to winning the Second Division by a huge margin. In his second, back in the top flight of the league, he would lead them to eighth out of 22 teams. In his third, he would end up lifting the English First Division Championship.

In short, everything changed with Ron Yeats as captain.

Yeats went on to play 417 games for Liverpool as captain, only being surpassed by Steven Gerrard decades later. He captained the club to two league titles, one FA Cup and a Division Two championship.

Ron Yeats was the turning point.

BACKBONE

Second Division champions

The Liverpool team that gained promotion from the Second Division to the First Division in the 1961–62 season was led by one of the great Scottish football managers of all time.

Bill Shankly.

And it was not just the Scotsman in the dugout who got Liverpool back to the top flight of the English game that season. There were Scottish players, too.

There's an idea in football that you need a strong spine down your team – a backbone – to win anything. In 1961–62 that spine was all Scottish:

Bert Slater in goal, signed from Falkirk.

Ron Yeats, a colossus in the defence, signed from Dundee United.

Tommy Leishman, a midfielder, from St Mirren.

Ian St John, a forward, from Motherwell.

TOM PALMER

Bill Shankly's team were promoted with five games to spare. And in the 60 or more years since, Scottish players have been at the heart of a lot of Liverpool's success: Steve Nicol, Kenny Dalglish, Gary McAllister, Graeme Souness, Alan Hansen and Andy Robertson, to name a few.

THE BIGGEST TOILET IN LIVERPOOL

Bill Shankly arrives

In 1959, Bill Shankly joined Liverpool as manager. To understand what he achieved, read the previous 86 entries in this book. The trophies, the players, the legacy – it's all there. Each page that comes before this one has been a consequence of Shankly's impact on the club as manager.

But how did he do it?

Bill Shankly was a revolutionary in football. A different kind of man. He did things that managers take for granted now, but did not then.

1. He insisted the manager should pick the team, not a selection committee in a boardroom.
2. He cut a squad of 38 almost in half, to a small, focused group of players.
3. He retained the previous manager's backroom team, rather than sweeping out the old. Two of

those men – Bob Paisley and Joe Fagan – would be instrumental in future successes.
4. He invested in Anfield, having named it 'the biggest toilet in Liverpool' and he improved the Melwood training ground, understanding that you won games through proper training.
5. He trained his players to be extremely fit – not a priority in those days.

The rest is history. A long history of unprecedented glory in the English game.

AFTER THE WAR

English champions # 5

The first full season of football resumed in August 1946, a year after the end of the Second World War.

It must have been a poignant moment for the players, back from fighting around the world – and for fans too, perhaps with missing family members who had stood beside them on the Kop.

Many people did not survive the war. Those killed in their homes as Liverpool was bombed. Those away fighting who never came home.

One Liverpool player in that first season back was Bob Paisley, who had served in North Africa and Italy during World War II, significantly helping to defeat fascism before returning to his passion: football. Paisley would later become Liverpool's most successful manager.

The season was tight. By the last few games, any

of four teams could still win the league title. But there were lots of games to cram in after a terrible winter's weather that had meant many games needed restaging well into the summer.

On 26 May 1947, Manchester United went top of the league with a 6–2 win. Five days later, third-place Liverpool went to second-place Wolverhampton Wanderers. The winner of that game would go above Manchester United. The loser would finish third or fourth.

Liverpool won.

But there was still one game to play. A full two weeks later, Stoke City played Sheffield United. If Stoke won, they would leapfrog all three teams at the top and win the league.

Stoke lost. Two-one.

And Liverpool became champions of England for the fifth time.

LIVERPOOL'S GREATEST MOMENTS

ENGLISH LEAGUE DIVISION ONE, 1946–47								
	P	W	D	L	F	A	GD	Pts
Liverpool	42	25	7	10	84	52	+32	57
Man United	42	22	12	8	95	54	+41	56
Wolves	42	25	6	11	98	56	+42	56
Stoke City	42	24	7	11	90	53	+37	55

ENGLISH CHAMPIONS # 4

Liverpool began the 1922–23 football season looking to win a second league title on the trot under the management of David Ashworth.

Then – in February 1923 – Ashworth resigned as Liverpool manager, moving on to take charge of Oldham Athletic, who were bottom of the First Division.

It was a strange choice for a football manager to make. To leave the English league champions – who would win it again that season – and join a club destined for the drop.

But as Liverpool manager for two-thirds of the 1922–23 season, Ashworth deserves some credit for his team's league win, even if he was no longer there by then.

It would be Ashworth's second spell managing Oldham. He had managed the club from 1906 until the outbreak of the First World War. He must have felt a strong emotional attachment to the club, for him to leave Liverpool on the brink of a second consecutive league title.

Liverpool won the title by six points (when it was still two points for a win). Players like Elisha Scott and Ephraim Longworth played all or most games for the club that year, while the leading scorer was Harry Chambers with 22.

ENGLISH LEAGUE DIVISION ONE, 1922–23								
	P	W	D	L	F	A	GD	Pts
Liverpool	42	26	8	8	70	31	+39	60
Sunderland	42	22	10	10	72	54	+18	54
Huddersfield	42	21	11	10	60	32	+28	53

GREAT SCOTT

English Champions # 3

When Liverpool won their third English Championship in 1921–22, they did it by conceding only 36 goals. This was typical of Liverpool's form in the 1920s – they were always one of the teams to concede fewer goals.

This was because they had a solid defence, and in goal, someone that Everton legend – Dixie Dean – called the greatest keeper he had faced:

Liverpool's Elisha Scott.

Scott was famous for training hard, walking more than three miles each way from home, refusing to catch the tram. And for obsessively testing his reflexes by throwing a ball against an uneven wall and catching the rebound.

Scott missed only three games in Liverpool's two league championship-winning seasons of 1921–22 and

1922–23. In the end he played for the club 468 times between 1912 and 1934.

ENGLISH LEAGUE DIVISION ONE, 1921–22								
	P	W	D	L	F	A	GD	Pts
Liverpool	42	22	13	7	63	36	+27	57
Spurs	42	21	9	12	65	39	+26	51
Burnley	42	22	5	15	72	54	+18	49

HOW THE KOP WAS MADE

English champions # 2

The 1905–06 English league championship was won by Liverpool in a tight contest with Preston North End. The two teams competed for the top spot and Liverpool finally took pole position in March 1906 with a 2–1 win at Preston's ground, Deepdale. They would keep that position until the end of the season.

The league win was hugely significant for the future of Liverpool F.C. and its ever-growing fanbase.

Because the league win had attracted such large crowds, there was extra revenue. That's money. Keen to grow the club and allow more fans in to enjoy the club's future, the owners decided to use that money to create a new stand.

The stand was named after a 1900 battle during the Boer War – the battle of Spion Kop, a steep hill.

A battle where many local men – from the Lancashire Regiment – lost their lives.

The Kop.

ENGLISH LEAGUE DIVISION ONE, 1905–06								
	P	W	D	L	F	A	GD	Pts
Liverpool	38	23	5	10	79	46	+33	51
Preston	38	17	13	8	54	39	+15	47
Sheffield Wednesday	38	18	8	12	63	52	+11	44

BOUNCING BACK

Promoted # 3

In 1904, four years after being crowned league champions for the first time Liverpool were relegated back to the second division. They had suffered a tough season during 1903–04, conceding 62 goals.

So manager Tom Watson – desperate to get the club back into the top flight – called on his old keeper from his glory days in the north-east of England.

Ned Doig was 37 years and 11 months old when Watson signed him. But it turned out to be a masterstroke. Signing the Scotsman to Liverpool led to a more focused defence in the 1904–05 season, meaning that only 25 goals were conceded in 34 games.

Up front things went well too for Liverpool, with 93 goals scored – the majority by three forwards: Robbie Robinson (24), Jack Parkinson (20) and Sam

Raybould (19).

After only one year away, Liverpool were promoted back to the top flight. And they would be ready for success this time.

ENGLISH LEAGUE DIVISION ONE, 1904–05								
	P	W	D	L	F	A	GD	Pts
Liverpool	34	27	4	3	93	25	+68	58
Bolton	34	27	2	5	87	32	+55	56
Man United	34	24	5	5	81	30	+51	53

THE FIRST CHAMPIONS

Champions # 1

At the end of the 1900–01 season, less than 10 years after Liverpool F.C. came into existence, they became champions of England.

To achieve that, they employed an already extremely successful manager. Tom Watson had won the league with Sunderland three times in the 1890s. He knew what success tasted like, and he was about to serve that to Liverpool fans.

It was the first – but not the last – example of Liverpool F.C. going out to get the best manager they could, to achieve what they wanted.

In the same season that Queen Victoria's death changed the history of England, so the history of football changed as Liverpool won their first league championship.

Winning 9 of their last 12 games, Liverpool sealed

it with a 1–0 victory at West Bromwich Albion. That meant they finished two points above Watson's old team, Sunderland.

It was a time before bus top parades, but, even so, when the Liverpool team arrived back home with the trophy, they were mobbed at the railway station and were celebrated by the fans as they travelled up Bold Street and Church Street.

Could Liverpool have imagined that 119 years later, in 2020, they would be winning their 19th league title?

ENGLISH LEAGUE DIVISION ONE, 1900–01								
	P	W	D	L	F	A	GD	Pts
Liverpool	34	19	7	8	59	35	+24	45
Sunderland	34	15	13	6	57	26	+31	43
Notts County	34	18	4	12	54	46	+8	40

REBOUND

Promoted #2

After the deep disappointment of being relegated back to Division Two in their first season in the top flight, Liverpool bounced back in extraordinary fashion. It was 1895–96.

They scored 106 goals in 30 games. This included home wins of 10–1, 7–1 and three 6–1 home victories, plus two 7–0 away wins.

The league table finished like this:

ENGLISH LEAGUE DIVISION TWO, 1895–96								
	P	W	D	L	F	A	GD	Pts
Liverpool	30	22	2	6	106	32	+74	46
Man City	30	21	4	5	63	38	+25	46

But, in 1896, it was not enough for Liverpool to finish top of the league. There was a series of playoffs with the teams from the bottom of Division One. These were known as Test Matches.

Liverpool played Small Heath (the precursor of Birmingham City), winning 4–0 at home and drawing 0–0 away. Then they won 2–0 at home to West Brom, but lost 2–0 away.

It was enough for Liverpool to be promoted for the second time in their history. Once again, they were among the elite. And, before long, they would be top of the elite.

TO THE TOP FLIGHT

Promoted # 1

Liverpool were promoted to the top flight of English football in 1894, during their second season and their first in the Football League. They had been admitted to the football league in 1893 because of their success in the Lancashire League and because Accrington and Bootle had resigned the league.

Their first game of the 1893–94 season resulted in a win against Middlesbrough Ironopolis. The scorer of the club's first league goal was Malcolm McVean.

With 12 of their 18 squad players hailing from Scotland, Liverpool won 22 out of 28 games and – in drawing the other six – went undefeated throughout the whole season.

But even this was still not enough for them to be promoted. They needed to play in a so-called Test match to go up.

LIVERPOOL'S GREATEST MOMENTS

Liverpool's first important final or playoff game in April 1894 would be against a team called Newton Heath. In 1902 that team would be renamed Manchester United.

Liverpool won. Two-nil. They were in the top flight for the first time.

LANCASHIRE'S FINEST

Lancashire League Champions # 1

Liverpool played their first full season, 1892–93, as a football team in the Lancashire League.

They started off with an 8–0 victory against Higher Walton with Scotsman, John Smith, registering the club's first goal in a league season.

Smith was one of 16 Scottish footballers in the Liverpool squad of 20 players. The other four were English and, between them, only managed six appearances in total.

Two hundred fans watched their first game, but by the end of the season, attendances were up to 2,000.

Liverpool won 17 of their 22 games, losing three, twice to Blackpool. But because Liverpool had a better goal ratio, Liverpool won their first championship – albeit the Lancashire League.

LANCASHIRE LEAGUE FINAL TABLE, 1892–93 *								
	P	W	D	L	F	A	GD	Pts
Liverpool	22	17	2	3	66	19	+47	36
Blackpool	22	17	2	3	82	31	+51	36

*Liverpool finished top because they had a higher goal ratio, and goal difference didn't count that season.

THE FIRST MERSEYSIDE DERBY

22 April 1893

The first time Liverpool and Everton came up against each other on a football pitch was as controversial as you'd hope any local derby would be.

It was the final of the Lancashire Senior Cup. And in Liverpool's first full season, destiny had put Liverpool and Everton in the final. Two teams who already had a divisive history.

The game was played at a neutral ground, up the road in Bootle.

After half an hour, Liverpool took the lead, through Tom Wylie. Now – as the game grew fiercer and fiercer – both teams went for it. A goal was disallowed. A shot was cleared off the line. The fans were as wound up as the players. The atmosphere was building to boiling point.

And then – in the last minute – Everton claimed a

handball in the penalty area. They wanted a penalty. The referee talked to his linesman and said no to Everton. There was outrage.

So the final score was Liverpool 1 Everton 0.

The Lancashire Senior Cup was not presented to Liverpool at the end of the game. The football authorities decided it would make the Everton players and fans so cross to present Liverpool with the trophy they had won, that it was presented a few days later at Liverpool's next game.

Everton sent a letter to the football authorities to complain about the referee. The authorities rejected the complaint and sent a letter of their own, accusing Everton of poor conduct and poor sportsmanship in the face of defeat.

LIVERPOOL F.C.'S FIRST GAME

Game one

The first game Liverpool F.C. ever played was a friendly against Rotherham Town.

There was a problem, however. It was 5:30 p.m. on 1 September 1892 at the same time and on the same night that Everton had a game too – against Bolton, at their new ground, Goodison Park.

The local newspapers had speculated which team would attract the bigger crowd. Who would the football fans of the city want to watch?

The answer was Everton, with 10,000 fans watching them. For Liverpool, it was only a few hundred.

But those who went to Anfield witnessed a 7–1 victory over Rotherham. They were at their team's first game. And no doubt, their children and grandchildren and great-grandchildren and great-great-

LIVERPOOL'S GREATEST MOMENTS

grandchildren will have been among the fans to watch six European champion teams and 20 English champions teams.

THE BADGE

The Liverpool F.C. badge has changed over the years, but one thing it has always displayed is the Liver Bird, the symbol of the city of Liverpool.

In 1892 – the year of the club's formation – the very first Liverpool F.C. badge had the bird on it. It also bore the Greek gods, Triton and Neptune, on account of Liverpool being very much a city of the sea.

The words on the 21st century badge are 'You'll Never Walk Alone'. But in the 19th century the wording was in Latin:

'Deus nobis haec otia fecit'

In English that means:

'God has granted us this ease'

Take from that what you will...

THE FORMATION OF LIVERPOOL F.C.

1892

Liverpool F.C. were formed because of an argument. An argument between the Everton committee and the owner of Anfield, where Everton played.

Yes, Everton used to play at Anfield!

But that was to change.

It was 12 March 1892, and the Everton committee had a meeting with their landlord, a Mr John Houlding.

Put simply, Houlding wanted Everton to pay more rent for the prime piece of land that was Anfield. It was a special place, after all, and it was felt that Everton should pay what it was worth.

But Everton refused to pay. That day Everton F.C. left Anfield and would only ever return as an away team.

That left John Houlding with a problem. What did

he do with what is now the most celebrated 1.6 acres of Merseyside land?

He decided to found a new football club.

He did so three days later, on 15 March 1892.

That football team would be called Liverpool F.C.

Read on for a sneak preview of another brilliant football story by Tom Palmer. . .

Football's Greatest Moments

Available now!

PERFECT ENDING

The argument about who is the greatest footballer that ever lived intensified as Lionel Messi's brilliant career evolved. Here was a man who had won the Ballon D'Or, the award for the year's greatest male footballer, seven times. But Messi had never lifted the World Cup. Could he be compared to Pelé and Maradona, football geniuses who had lifted the ultimate prize?

Messi was 35 when his last chance came: Qatar 2022. After unthinkably losing their opening game to Saudi Arabia, Messi's Argentina went on to beat Mexico, Poland, Australia, the Netherlands and Croatia. Now they faced the reigning champions, France, in the World Cup final. The two teams were so evenly matched that 90 minutes and extra time could not separate them. The winners of the 2022 men's World Cup – and Messi's legacy – would be decided on penalties.

Argentina needed to score with their last kick.

Messi waited with his teammates, a row of blue and white stripes, to see if he and they would achieve the ultimate stamp of greatness... or not.

GOOOOOOAAAAAALLLLLLLLLL!

The world changed in a moment. The penalty went in. The crowd roared. Most of the Argentina players rushed forward. But Lionel Messi dropped to his knees. On seeing him, his teammates doubled back, their arms encircling their captain, as every Argentina fan's arms encircled him in spirit. Maybe every football fan's.

Because those fans had just witnessed one of the greatest moments in football.

LIONEL MESSI	
Born	1987, Argentina
Position	Forward
Club goals	737
International goals	109
Selected honours	La Liga (10 times); Champion's League (4 times); World Cup

THE PERFECT BEGINNING

Pelé was at the beginning of his career when he played in his first World Cup final, against Sweden in 1958. The youngest player to play in the greatest game, he scored twice.

Pelé was just 17.

His first goal was one of the most outrageous goals ever scored in a World Cup final. The ball looped over to him from the left as he broke into the penalty area. He chested it down, beating the first defender. But a second defender closed him down, meaning he didn't have the space to shoot. So he chipped the ball over the Swede and, without allowing the ball to touch the ground, volleyed it into the back of the net.

His second goal came in the 90th minute, a deft header securing a 5–2 win and Brazil's first World Cup. Pelé had scored six goals during the tournament: one in the quarter-final, three in the semi, and now two in the final.

When the final whistle blew, he passed out, came round, then wept for joy. Pelé had become, and would remain, Brazil's greatest male footballer. In all, he would play in four World Cup tournaments, helping his country to win it three times: 1958, 1962 and 1970.

PELÉ	
Born	1940, Brazil
Position	Forward
Club goals	709
International goals	77
Selected honours	World Cup (3 times); FIFA Player of the Century

MARTA'S FIFTH

When the Brazilian footballer, Marta, won the FIFA World Player of the Year in 2010, she became the only footballer to win the ultimate individual award five years on the trot, dominating the award from 2006 to 2010 – something Messi, Pelé and Maradona did not achieve. Then she won it again in 2018.

She was clearly the greatest ever female footballer. Playing professional football in Sweden, the USA and Brazil, Marta had an impossible combination of speed, power, touch and intelligence. She had everything.

Marta was the first to score in five World Cup final tournaments, an achievement matched only recently by Ronaldo in the men's World Cup. Her records and awards could fill a book on their own.

Although she was part of the Olympic Games winning team twice in 2004 and 2008, she never lifted the World Cup.

Nevertheless, Marta's fifth consecutive FIFA award is undoubtedly still one of the greatest moments in football. And it came at a time that women's football and footballers were emerging from a time of unfair treatment.

MARTA	
Born	1986, Brazil
Position	Forward
Club goals	182
International goals	119
Selected honours	FIFA World Player of the Year (6 times)

POWER

When Scotland played England in 1881 at Easter Road, Edinburgh, 1,000 fans showed up to watch. But the newspaper coverage was full of contempt and focused on the players' clothes and bodies, not the football action.

It was a game between women.

The newspapers barely mentioned the great historical moment of the first women's game under the rules of association football, nor that Scotland beat England 3–0 in the first women's international football match. It was a time long before social media and the internet. The men who wrote and published newspapers could tell the story just how they wanted.

The teams played again in Glasgow a week later and – wound up by the newspapers – men invaded the pitch and rioted, throwing objects at the players, forcing the game to be stopped.

A third game was cancelled.

There are records of more games between Scottish and English teams over this period, but little was written about it in the newspapers and little evidence remains. History is in the hands of those who have the power. Until those who have the power changes.

INTERNATIONAL FRIENDLY	
Saturday, 7 May 1881	
Scotland Ladies 3–0 England Ladies	
Lily St Clair	
Louise Cole	
Maud Randford	

TAKING THE KNEE

In 2016 the US footballer Megan Rapinoe put her career as an international footballer at risk. She 'took the knee' – in other words, she knelt during the playing of the American national anthem, rather than standing to attention, as was the tradition.

She did this to protest against the treatment of Black people by the police in the USA and to protest against racism generally.

Rapinoe used her fame and profile through football to make this protest. Rapinoe was the highest profile footballer in the USA and the most famous female footballer in the world. She could have been dropped by her club and country just for taking the knee.

Rapinoe had spoken about taking the knee. She says that white athletes don't feel the effects of the racism and that – even if it is not their fault – they, like everyone, all have the responsibility to challenge what is wrong.

HISTORICAL WRONG

The first Black player to be selected to play for the England men's team was a high-scoring Plymouth forward called Jack Leslie.

But he was dropped from the England team before the game took place.

Later in his life he remarked – in an interview and as an explanation – that 'they must have forgot I was a coloured boy'.

It was 1925. Leslie had been scoring a goal every three games for Plymouth and had come to the team selectors' attention. But – as he said – it is very likely that as soon as the Football Association became aware he was Black, he was removed from the team.

In 2022 a statue was put up at Plymouth's stadium, Home Park. In the same year the Football Association awarded Jack Leslie, who had died in 1988, the international cap he never received. Ninety-seven years later.